ONE CHRISTMAS ANGEL

ONE CHRISTMAS ANGEL

One Unique Christmas Angel, Handcrafted by a Child,
Brings Joy to Two Romances

PAMELA GRIFFIN
TAMELA HANCOCK MURRAY

BARBOUR
PUBLISHING

Published by Barbour Publishing, Inc., P.O. Box 719, Uhrichsville, Ohio 44683, www.barbourbooks.com

Our mission is to publish and distribute inspirational products offering exceptional value and biblical encouragement to the masses.

Member of the
Evangelical Christian
Publishers Association

Printed in the United States of America.
5 4 3 2 1

Strawberry Angel

by Pamela Griffin

Dedication

To all those who helped by critiquing this,
I extend a huge thank-you, especially to Mom
(who went above and beyond)!
A special note of appreciation goes to Sally Daniels
and shelter director Brenda Jackson (www.bwf1.com)
for their help regarding the subject of women's shelters.
And to my boys, Brandon and Joshua—
I sure enjoyed making the angel crafts with you for this book!
Thanks for being my two special guys.
As always, I dedicate this story to my patient Lord,
who's often worked through my foolish and embarrassing
blunders to the benefit of others—
revealing His glory in the process.

Chapter 1

Noelle surmised that the addition of one more December birthday to lump with her previous twenty-two must have caused her brain to flip—or fry. After all, what idiot would take on a hair-dying job the day of a fund-raising banquet?

She would.

With only four hours to go until the big event, Noelle rushed to make it on time, but she wanted classy, dark auburn hair to go with the new bronze velvet evening dress she'd nabbed at a warehouse sale last week. Mousy brown just didn't cut it for her, and this had been the first opportunity she'd had to color her hair since she'd needed to work overtime at Odds & Ends Craft Supplies the past several days.

She groped for an oversized towel and threw it over her

rinsed head. To avoid having any smelly fumes irritate her eyes, she kept them squeezed shut as she'd done throughout most of the process. Twisting the velour towel turban-style, she straightened from the sink. Steam still covered the mirror, so she couldn't see her image. She looked down at her hands and noticed the maroon polish on her nails had chipped. Great. One more thing for her to do.

Over the loud whir of the exhaust fan, a knock sounded at the front door of her duplex. She stopped rummaging through a shoe box of half-filled glass bottles containing a wide spectrum of nail polishes. What was that rule about being busy in the bathroom and the phone or doorbell ringing?

She slipped her glasses on and headed for the door, casting a glance at her baggy, gray, water-splotched sweat suit. It was probably just Shannon. Her neighbor had a habit of popping over unannounced. Noelle swung the door wide, expecting to see Shannon's elfin features.

Instead, rich cocoa-brown eyes in the handsome face of a deliveryman stared back. Impulsively, Noelle clapped a hand over the towel mound to keep it in place, her mind refusing to believe what her still burning eyes clearly showed her.

"Hi," he said, his voice smooth. "I have a package for you. I'll need you to sign for it."

Noelle's heart jumped. This could not be happening! Avoiding his curious stare, she accepted the stylus and poised her hand above the electronic keyboard where he pointed, putting her other hand to the bottom of the gadget he held to help keep it steady.

Her weighty towel began to topple backward. Trying to prevent its further downslide, she hunched her shoulders and scrunched her head lower, like a turtle retreating into its shell. But gravity was having its way.

"Sorry—I'll just be a second." She thrust the stylus and electronic keyboard at him, minus her signature, and partially closed the door, so he couldn't see her. She wished she could ooze into the tufts of sand-colored carpet and disappear.

Todd Brentley—the guy for whom she would have gladly given away all her teen idol magazines in tenth grade for just one date—stood on the other side of her door. And here she stood in matted, fuzzy blue slippers, with unmade face and wet hair hidden in a towel—and wearing her sloppiest clothes to boot!

She whipped the towel off and bent at the waist to retie it around her head. Vivid pink hair—not auburn—streamed down in wet clumps before her eyes.

"Agh!" She gave a strangled cry.

A tap sounded on the door. "Miss, you all right in there?"

Noelle shot to a standing position, wet hair slinging into her face. "Don't come in! I'm fine. I—I'll be right with you."

Gulping in a breath, she tried to think. She had no idea what had gone wrong, but she couldn't very well stand here and dwell on this latest calamity now, not with Todd perched on her doorstep. She swept the loathsome hair back, slapped the towel over her head like a hood, and clutched it under her chin. Determined to act as calm as possible under the circumstances, she swung the door open.

Todd turned from staring at the boxwoods that flanked the duplex. "Everything okay?"

"Terrific. Would you mind holding that thing steady while I sign?"

He gave a puzzled grin. "Sure. I always do. Sorry I caught you at a bad time."

"That's okay." She was surprised that she wrote her name legibly and the electronic signature didn't look too much like chicken scratch from the way her hand was shaking—though with these computer contraptions the delivery company used, her signature always managed to look like a second grader's who'd just started penmanship. Tacking on what she hoped passed for a smile, she handed the stylus back to him.

His gaze was plastered to her forehead, with something close to horrified fascination. "Thanks. Here's your package," he said, not looking away from that spot.

"Thank you." Noelle snatched the box from him.

He seemed to collect himself and gave her one of his dissolve-your-knees-into-puddles smiles, his teeth as white and even as always. "Have a nice holiday."

"You, too." Noelle backed into her apartment and shut the door, exhaling a relieved breath. Unable to resist, she hurried to the window and peeked through a chink in the cream-colored curtains, watching as Todd sauntered toward his brown delivery truck. Looking down at the electronic device in his hand, he suddenly stopped.

"Oh no," Noelle whispered as he turned, gave her door a probing glance, then strode back up the sidewalk, his long-legged gait quickly eating up the distance.

He remembered.

Noelle listened for the inevitable knock, praying she would make it through the rest of this afternoon without tearing her hair out.

On second thought, that might not be such a bad idea.

When the swift rap came, she stayed as still as a cardinal hiding from a curious cat, hoping he would just go away and think her busy in the back room. She should have remembered his stubborn streak. After his third knock, she tossed what she assumed to be her father's Christmas gift onto the sofa and crammed the errant strand that stuck to her forehead as far back as it would go beneath the towel. She inched open the door, putting her eye to the crack. "Yes?"

"Sorry to bother you," he said, his brow crinkling in a cute, boyish way, "but I was wondering if you're the same Noelle Sanders I went to Omega High with. The package said 'N. L. Sanders,' and you signed your name as Noelle. Not a very common name. At least, I don't think it is."

He rubbed a hand along the back of his neck, looking uncertain. It struck her as odd that the most popular guy in her graduating class could feel such a thing as embarrassment. Yet as much as she would prefer to remain anonymous, she couldn't lie.

"I went to Omega High," she admitted through the fraction of space between door and lintel.

A hundred-watt smile lit his face. "I thought you looked familiar! I'm Todd. Todd Brentley. You sat behind me in Art Appreciation during our sophomore and junior years. You helped me with my homework, too. Remember?"

How could she forget? Noelle nodded and reluctantly opened the door wider. She'd spent most of the time in class staring dreamily at his broad shoulders covered by his letter jacket and noticing how the fluorescent light picked out red highlights in his mahogany-dark hair—instead of concentrating on the teacher. Despite her eagerness to help by tutoring him with his English and aiding him in art, her own disappointing overall grade of a B-minus that semester had reflected her inattentiveness.

"So what are you doing back in Hartford Falls?" he asked, breaking into her thinking balloon. "I heard you'd come home."

"I found I prefer small-town life."

"Really? Maybe some afternoon we could get together and talk over old times."

"Sure." She politely smiled, doubting he would follow through.

"Well, I guess I'd better hit the road." Todd's gaze went to her toweled head. "You look busy, and I've got plenty of deliveries to make. Christmas rush, you know."

"Yeah. See you around."

After Todd drove off with a farewell wave, Noelle made a beeline for her bedroom to assess the damage. With the minutes growing scanter, she wasn't sure what to do.

Pulling off the towel, she glared at her pink-topped image in the dresser mirror. She grabbed the bottle of hair coloring standing next to a box with dark auburn curls pictured on front, and scanned the bottle's label. Nothing. She turned it over and saw a name printed on the bottom. PINK FUSION. *Not* Auburn Sunset. This bottle did not match that box. Someone had switched them.

Her first impulse to call the drugstore was eclipsed when she saw the time. Her complaint would have to wait until tomorrow. Less than three hours remained for her to figure out what to wear. She toyed with the idea of staying home, but she couldn't do that to her best friend, Cindy, who'd organized the event. But one thing was certain; bronze velvet did not go with Pink Fusion.

Todd thought about Noelle as he made the rest of his deliveries for the afternoon. When he'd transmitted the delivery information to the centralized database with his handheld DIAD while walking back to his truck, he had really looked at her signature on the screen for the first time—and realized then who she was.

He'd heard that she worked for a lucrative advertising firm in the Big Apple and wondered what had happened to cause her to return to their small town. According to his mom, the firm had planned to give Noelle a promotion, before she up and quit her job without explanation. Now she worked at a craft store and volunteered at the local women's shelter which her friend Cindy directed. Seemed a step down for her to work retail, but he did admire her generosity in helping out at the shelter.

One thing about his mom, she was a wealth of information. Even if her news did border on gossip at times, Todd was grateful for the info he'd collected about Noelle. She still seemed a bit zany, but it was her zaniness that made him smile. Like when he didn't get the football scholarship his senior year because of an injury on the field that resulted in him never being able to play football again. Noelle had come alone to visit him at the hospital, holding a bouquet of helium balloons on which she'd drawn silly faces. The entire time, she'd cracked jokes and made her own silly faces to get him to laugh. And he had. Neither his family nor his other classmates and friends who'd visited had been able to extract more than a weak smile from him. But Noelle had made him laugh.

Todd glanced at his watch. Only one hour until curtain time and the role he'd promised Mom he would take on for the cause. He wondered if Noelle would be at the banquet and grinned at the thought of seeing her again. Too bad he hadn't thought to ask her earlier.

Exiting her car, Noelle was careful not to step on the hem of her rose-colored dress. Her brand-new dress still hung in her closet, waiting for an event when her hair didn't clash with the bronze velvet. She slammed the door shut, grimacing when her faint image reflected in the dark window. Well, there was nothing to do but grit her teeth, smile, and make the best of things. Because of the holiday season, both salons in town were booked solid through New Year's Eve. Even though she'd begged, no hair stylist had an opening to take her and try to fix the bad dye job, though a receptionist had taken her name in case a customer canceled. So she'd crammed her pink locks into a loose style atop her head and hoped for the best.

Noelle hurried through the crowded convention center parking lot and pulled open the heavy glass door. A glittery sign on a pedestal at the entrance pointed the way to the grand ballroom. Her heels sank into spongy blue carpet as she rushed through the double doors of the enormous area.

Spotting her mother near a table catty-cornered to the large stage, Noelle darted by the edge of the milling crowd, hoping to make herself as inconspicuous as possible on the way to greet her. This corner of the room was semi-dark, the high brass chandelier in the middle of the carved ceiling above the dance floor the only source of light. And that light was thankfully dimmed.

"Noelle! There you are. Wow, girl, what've you done to your hair?"

Obviously not dimmed enough.

Noelle faced her friend, Cindy, with a forced smile. "Interesting, isn't it?"

A short, blond man stood by Cindy's side. His gaze

bounced up to Noelle's upswept hair, then down to her satin floor-length gown and up again.

"Hmm," Cindy murmured, "well you've outdone yourself this time, that's for sure. It's pretty though. You look sort of. . .Christmasy."

"Thanks," Noelle said with a grimace.

Cindy grinned, her own ivory lace dress complementing her cocoa-dark skin and shining, straight black hair. "Let me take your coat. I'll put it with mine in the closet behind the stage. Oh, and you'd better let your mother know you're here. She was searching for you earlier."

Noelle shrugged out of her fake white fur and handed it to her friend. "It looks like a good turnout. You should raise a sizeable amount for the home with this crowd."

Cindy's smile turned into a full-fledged grin. "Yeah, I'm surprised at the number of people from out of town who showed up—like Diamond Jim in the Stetson over there. And your mother's idea should be the crowning touch."

Noelle looked away from the heavyset man with the diamonds flashing from his fingers, wristwatch, and tie tack. "What idea?"

"You mean she didn't tell you? Well, you'll see soon enough. I have to go show Paul, here, the ropes. He's agreed to be in charge of the dinner music and change out the CDs. You probably haven't heard, but Will fell off a ladder this morning. His leg's in a cast. The band had to cancel."

"You're kidding!"

"I wish I was. I don't know who's going to finish building that set for our play, what with Will laid up and Christmas coming in less than four weeks. You can still direct the kids, of course. You don't really need a stage for that. By the way, excuse my bad manners. This is Paul Reily. He's new in town. Paul, Noelle Sanders."

He gave a short nod, and Noelle managed a smile before Cindy whisked him away toward a sound system near the stage.

Bracing herself, Noelle joined her mother at the front. Her mom's soft peach cashmere dress was perfect for her slender build and blended beautifully with her ash-blond hair. She appeared professional yet elegant at the same time.

"Hi, Mom. Your daughter's here."

Her mother turned from talking with a tall, silver-haired gentleman. "Oh!" she exclaimed when she saw Noelle, her ready smile slipping into a stare of disbelief.

Excusing herself from the distinguished-looking man, she grabbed Noelle's elbow and led her to a long table covered with a cranberry red tablecloth and white lace overlay, one of many throughout the room. Out of hearing distance of the others, her mom lit right into her. "You weren't kidding on the phone earlier. It really is Pink Fusion. What possessed you to dye your hair today of all days?"

Noelle felt as if her smile had frozen. She was surprised it hadn't cracked yet. "And a lovely evening to you, too, Mother."

Her mom gave an exasperated click of her tongue. "Your personal holiday makeovers almost always end in disaster—haven't you learned that yet? The colored contacts last year were bad enough when you lost one at the Christmas party and had to walk around with one green eye and one purple eye. But this! And wherever did you get that dress?" Her pained gaze scanned Noelle from head to toe.

"Oh, this old thing?" Noelle quipped. "Surely you remember when I was a bridesmaid in Lisa's wedding?"

"That was. . .four years ago. And in the spring, too." For a moment, her mother looked as if she might need to sit down. She eyed the short bell sleeves. "Aren't you cold?"

"It's crowded in here, and they do have central heating. This was all I could come up with on short notice. But I did wear my coat. I mean, I'm not completely loopy or anything." She gave a clipped laugh.

The look her mother sent questioned that statement. "At least the rose color does complement your hair," she amended. "And all that pink is pretty with your green eyes."

Noelle groaned. "Mother, please."

"Never mind. What's done is done. This is where you're to sit." Her mom gestured to one of the colorful place settings. A gilded name card sat propped near the silver-trimmed china with NOELLE SANDERS written in gold script. Her mother's was to her right.

"The decorating committee did a great job." Noelle hung her white satin pillbox purse over the back of her chair. "By the way, Cindy said you'd planned a surprise of some sort—"

"Oh, now what," her mother interrupted. "Mrs. Michaels is trying to get my attention. I hope another problem hasn't arisen. Sorry, dear. I'd better go see what's wrong." She hurried off, leaving a cloud of vanilla musk in her wake.

Noelle sank to the upholstered chair and eased out of her too-tight shoes. Four years they'd sat in a shoe box tucked away with this dress. Her feet must have grown. Rubbing one stocking foot over the other under the hidden covering of the floor-length tablecloth, she scanned the dressed-to-the-hilt crowd. Hopefully this banquet would begin soon so she could eat, donate her offering, and go home.

The lights grew brighter. A dark-haired woman in a glittering, red sequined dress took the stage and walked up to a standing microphone. "Good evening, ladies and gentlemen. Cindy Grafton, the director of the shelter, has asked me to emcee tonight. I'm Charla, and we're so pleased that you've come to help support our cause."

Settling back, Noelle listened as Charla outlined Haven of Hope ministries, describing it as a nonprofit organization with one hundred percent of its donations going to the shelter. With a sweet smile that would cause the world's worst miser to unzip his money belt, she thanked everyone for attending. "I do apologize for the delay with the meal," she added, "but due to van trouble, the catering service is running late. So we've decided to hold the auction first."

Noelle jerked to attention. *Auction? What auction?*

"Thanks to an ingenious suggestion from a member of the town council, we've added a twist to things this year, like nothing we've ever done before." Charla beamed at the crowd. "You ladies should be particularly interested. Especially those needing strenuous work done around your homes or places of business. The kind of work that requires heavy, manual labor. The kind of work that men do best."

Men in black tuxes walked from one of the wings backstage and filed into a single line behind the announcer. Each wore a red carnation on his lapel.

"Tonight, we're auctioning off the services of fourteen of Hartford Falls's very own. Men who've kindly volunteered their muscle to help us raise money to build a new wing for Haven of Hope. And what muscles they have, eh, ladies?"

Amid the snickers circulating the crowd, Noelle groaned. *This had to be Mother's idea. Only she would think up something as corny—and embarrassing—as this.*

"So ladies get out your checkbooks. And, men, don't feel you can't join in on the fun, too. I'm sure some of you could use another pair of hands to help paint that house or work on the roof. Oh—and for those who don't wish to participate but still want to make a donation, envelopes are provided at the back for your convenience, on the brochure table. Just nab one of the committee members afterward to give them your contribution. That said, let the games begin!" With these final words, the announcer swung her hand upward in a lighthearted gesture.

The last two men strode onstage and took a place beside their peers, turning to face the crowd. Noelle gasped and clutched the tablecloth.

Todd Brentley stood at the end of the line. And he seemed to be looking straight at her.

Chapter 2

What's Todd doing here?

Noelle shook her head briskly, hoping the blood would flow back to her brain and she could think more clearly. Well, it was obvious what he was doing here, but why hadn't Mother told Noelle about this when she'd talked to her on the phone earlier? Surely she'd known.

Noelle compressed her lips. Oh, yes, she'd known. As chairwoman of the town council, her mother made it a point to be informed. And Noelle nurtured a sneaking suspicion of why her mother hadn't mentioned this tidbit to Noelle after her recounting of Todd's package delivery. She was trying to play matchmaker again. Anything to aid the cause of pairing off her daughter with a "nice boy" and get her married. On a hunch, Noelle glanced at the name card by the place setting to her left.

TODD BRENTLEY.

Noelle narrowed her eyes and sought her mother out in the crowd, while a woman exclaimed over winning the services of a landscaper to help with her garden. At last Noelle spotted the familiar peach dress. Her mother stood near the stage, watching the proceedings with rapt attention, a smile on her seemingly guileless face. Despairing of ever catching her mother's eye, Noelle swung her attention back to Todd.

A feast for the eyes was an understatement concerning this man. His black silk tux strained over broad shoulders. A crisp white shirt covered a lean but, she was certain, powerful chest. As if he'd just stepped in from outdoors, his dark hair had a sporty, windblown look. The stage lights picked up the twinkle in his eyes as he stared out over the crowd and gave them a good-natured grin.

Mel, Brad, Antonio—eat your heart out. Noelle vaguely listened as, one by one, the men were auctioned off—a grocer, a dentist, a construction worker, and more. But her attention never wavered from Todd.

Finally, it was his turn. Noelle watched as he took his place beside the announcer at the microphone, as the others had done. A sudden expression of interest shone on the emcee's face, and a cat's-got-the-cream smile formed on her red lips.

"I think I'll join in the bidding on this last round," Charla purred into the microphone. "I have chores needing done around the house. When a woman lives alone, the to-do list is constantly piling up." She let out a lilting laugh and lifted one scarlet nail into the air. "One hundred dollars."

Noelle bristled. Could she do that? Was the emcee even allowed to participate?

A chorus of frenzied bids rose around the room, increasing by twenty-five dollars each time. Heat flamed Noelle's cheeks. She was embarrassed for Todd, but mostly she was appalled by the behavior of her peers. Appalled and angry. Of the women who bid, Noelle recognized many as being single. They acted as if they'd never seen a man before.

Her focus swung back to Todd. Well, okay. Granted, they probably never had—not one like Todd Brentley anyway. Many men onstage were nice-looking, but Todd possessed charisma—always had. It probably had something to do with that breathtaking, boyish smile that could suddenly turn up to full power and light the room with a dazzling, melt-your-heart grin. Or maybe those velvety-brown eyes, full of mischief one moment, brimming with tenderness the next.

Charla bid again, topping the last offer of five hundred dollars.

Noelle shut her eyes. She couldn't watch any longer.

"One thousand dollars," a familiar, high-pitched voice sang out.

Noelle was going to die—then and there. If her heart beat any faster, it would jump out of her chest. Then again, that might be a blessing. At least death would remove her from this mortifying travesty.

Her mother wouldn't do this to her. She wouldn't. She may be responsible for a lot of things, but she wouldn't do this to her one and only daughter.

Noelle peeked one eye open to see her mother's peach cashmere sleeve lifted high in the air.

She would.

The exit sign over the fire escape door beckoned, only twenty or so feet away. Noelle could slip out of her chair and hurry to the door unnoticed. Right. Unnoticed—wielding a fluorescent beacon atop her head. Still it was worth a shot. This was worse than any measly fire. She considered it an emergency. By the time the alarms went off, she would be outside, racing away from this nightmare of a banquet. Of course, her coat was in a closet behind the stage, and the temperature had plummeted to the low twenties now that the sun was down.

"Congratulations, Mrs. Sanders," Charla said, voice resigned. "There doesn't seem to be any other bids. Todd Brentley is yours."

"And I have just the activity for him," Noelle's mother exclaimed. "One that will most certainly aid my daughter."

Noelle eyed the door again. What was a little cold air? Certainly no worse than being spotlighted in her mom's public matchmaking scheme. With her toes, she felt around for her satin pumps, found one, and quickly slid her foot inside, then searched for the other. Nothing but spongy carpet. She stretched her pointed toes further, holding on to the seat for balance, as her leg made a frantic sideways sweep for the missing shoe.

Nothing.

Desperate, Noelle dipped her head underneath the tablecloth and scanned the flowered expanse of carpet for the elusive rose satin slipper. Ah, there it was.

"Noelle, what are you doing?"

Startled by the suddenness of her mother's voice, Noelle shot up and bumped her head on the underside of the table.

"Ohhh," she groaned. Rubbing the sore spot, she awkwardly sat up—and gasped in shocked dismay.

Todd Brentley smiled down at her, obviously amused. "We meet again."

"Noelle," her mother's voice tinkled, as though the world

had not just ended, "you remember Todd Brentley, don't you? Well, dear, he's all yours!"

Todd had never seen anyone whose face matched her hair. Noelle reminded him of his aunt's artificial Christmas tree. Bright pink all over.

Her rose-colored lips opened as if she would say something, then closed. A thick, pink curl fell from the top of her head, hitting her dark fringe of lashes and brushing against her cheek. She swept the tendril away with the back of one hand.

Strawberry soda pop mixed with a scoop of vanilla ice cream. That's what her hair reminded him of. The color of his favorite dessert when he was a boy.

"I'll be leaving you two now," Mrs. Sanders said.

Noelle's head whipped her way. "Oh, but—Mother. You're not actually leaving?" Her tense smile matched her voice, hinging on desperation.

"Not the banquet, of course. But I should mingle with the guests. It's expected of me. I'll return when the meal is served."

"But—we really should talk about this—"

"There's no need to thank me, dear. I'm always glad to help aid your cause in any way I can." Mrs. Sanders smiled benevolently, though Todd detected mischief in her expression before she glided away.

He pulled out the chair next to Noelle and sat down. "Great turnout."

"Yes." Her attention flicked to a nearby exit door.

"I had no idea there were so many wealthy people in our area. And I thought I knew just about everyone in town."

"Some live in Manhattan and other big cities," she said slowly after lengthy seconds elapsed. "I broadcasted news of the event through the local media—newspapers, radio—as well as fliers in the mail." Noelle turned impossibly green eyes his way—a vibrant holly green. But it was the anxious expression in them that arrested his attention.

"You okay?"

Half her mouth twisted up. "Let's just say that judging from the way my day has progressed, the events of this evening shouldn't really surprise me." She reached for her water glass, her hand noticeably shaking.

He tried to decipher that odd statement, then gave up and shrugged. "Your mother explained your situation. Just tell me when you want me. I'm always ready to aid a worthy cause."

Noelle choked. Pulling the glass from her mouth, she coughed and doubled over. Concerned, Todd directed a couple of swift slaps to her back. She wasn't choking on anything but water, so nothing would be stuck in her windpipe.

He snatched a soft breadstick from a wicker basket nearby. "Here. This should help."

She shook her head, pushing away his offering. Her breathing returned to normal, but the narrowed, flashing eyes she shifted in his direction surprised him.

"Just to get things straight between us right from the start, let me tell you what I don't want, Todd Brentley." Her tone was quiet, seething with fire. "I don't want your pity. Just because she's my mother doesn't mean she always knows what's best for me. And in this case, she's sadly mistaken."

Baffled, Todd shook his head. "Sorry, but I'm at a loss as to how you think a thousand dollar contribution to the shelter could be a mistake." Actually he was at a loss about everything she'd said but didn't want to push his luck.

"That's not what I'm talking about."

"What else is there?"

"Nothing. Never mind. It's not important." She picked up her water glass, changed her mind when it was halfway to her mouth, and set it back down. She snatched up a breadstick, tearing off the end with her teeth.

Todd eyed the breadstick he still held and tossed it on his plate. Noelle kept her attention fixed on the crowd, the breadstick disappearing in swift, angry bites.

Might as well give it another try. After all, that's why he was here.

Todd cleared his throat. "Saturday evenings work best for me. Just call when it's convenient. With time running out, I'm sure you'll want to make it soon."

"Look," she cut in, her gaze piercing him like the sharp needles of an evergreen, "I don't think I made myself clear. If and when I do decide to date, I don't need any favors from you in 'aiding a worthy cause.' So you're off the hook. You owe me nothing for this crazy auction. Zip. Zero. Zilch." She flicked her hand in a dismissing gesture with each Z word.

Todd's mouth twitched at the corners. "Date?"

The indignation blazing in her eyes gave way to mounting horror. "You know. What you and I've been discussing for the past few minutes. What you said about calling you on a Saturday evening when it's convenient. . . ." Her words trailed off, reminding him of a squeaky little mouse. A cute mouse, though.

He shook his head. "A thousand dollars is pretty expensive to buy a date, Noelle. I'm flattered you think I'm worth it, but. . ."

Noelle groaned and dropped her head into her hands. She briskly massaged her temples and two more pink strands fell from the top. "A fire is child's play compared to this. I could run out that exit door and get away before they caught me."

Confused by her strange mumbling, Todd clarified. "Your mother mentioned that the guy building the set for the

Christmas play broke his leg. I'm supposed to take his place."

Noelle let out a short laugh. "Well, Cindy'll be relieved to hear that. I'm only in charge of advertising and directing the play. Cindy is the founder of the ministry, but then you probably already knew that. . .ohhh."

At her soft moan, Todd touched her shoulder. "You okay?"

"My pride is blown to smithereens, but what else is new?" She looked up. "I can't believe I thought—and said—what I did. You must think—well, I know what I'd think. You do, don't you?"

Surprised that he understood her garbled words, he took pity on her. "You want to know what I think?"

She shook her head no, then nodded yes, like an uncertain child who wants to please but is faced with a puzzling question. He hid a smile, putting his hand over hers. Her eyes widened, and his gut clenched.

"Well, here it is. I think you're the most interesting woman I've ever had the privilege of knowing, every pink inch of you. And I'm glad our paths crossed again."

His words made her feel better, as did his warm hand atop hers, but he could have left out the part about every pink inch of her. Also Noelle wondered about his definition of the word "interesting." She'd always heard the term used when one didn't want to hurt another's feelings: How do you like my new Mylar dress? Interesting. What did you think of your blind date? Interesting. Isn't this dribble-art wallpaper a scream? Interesting.

Then Todd's words hit full force. He was glad their paths had crossed again. Meaning—what? That he wanted to be with her?

Yeah, right, Noelle. Why would the most handsome, alluring guy at the banquet want to be seen with the freaky pink lady—a combination of nineties punk rocker and Barbie doll reject?

"Cat got your tongue?" He sounded amused.

"I think I've said too much already. I should save whatever face I have left."

"It's a nice face." Leaning back in his chair, he withdrew his hand from hers.

She missed the feel of it.

"Under the circumstances, your reaction is understandable, Noelle. Now that I think of it, I wouldn't welcome the idea of being bought as someone's date, like some sort of male escort. Seems cheap. I understand how you must have felt."

"Please, could we just drop the subject? There are apparently a number of things my mother chose not to reveal, such as her intention of bidding on you for building the Christmas set—which I'm grateful for, don't misunderstand me. But will you tell me something? Did she phone you about participating tonight and put you up to this?"

"No. My mom's a member of the committee, too. She's the one who talked me into it."

"Your mom's a member of the town council?" Another tidbit of information her mother had withheld.

"Yeah." Todd leaned close. "Listen. I'm starving and it doesn't appear as if the caterers are going to serve us any time soon." He picked up the breadstick from his plate. "I'm not all that crazy about a diet of bread and water, so how about we go grab a bite to eat and discuss the building project?"

"You mean just leave? Now?"

"The auction's ended, and I haven't eaten since lunch. I'm sure your mom wouldn't mind if you and I duck out for an hour or so."

No, you're right. She'll probably do flips for joy.

Todd grinned as though he could read her mind. "So how about it? Are you game?"

"Well. . ." Noelle studied the crowd, mingling again, though some were seated at their tables. Cindy faced Paul, with her hands upraised in obvious frustration. Noelle's mother laughed and talked with the mayor, who stood beside Diamond Jim. It seemed like a good time to escape. No one would miss her.

"Why not? I can spare an hour." Who was she kidding?

His offer sounded like a touch of gold from Midas. That would explain why everything suddenly seemed to glitter.

Todd collected her coat from backstage and helped her into it. Somehow they slipped out of the grand ballroom, unseen—without the aid of the fire escape.

Chapter 3

Noelle looked through the door of the all night mini-mart where Todd stood in line at the counter. He held a cardboard tray with what looked like two submarine sandwiches and paper cups of coffee. Her stomach turned over at the thought of food.

Feeling perspiration trickle down her sides and glad he'd left the keys in the ignition, she rolled down her car window a fraction. Most of the pins had slipped in her hair, so she plucked them out along with the huge clip, then pulled a brush through the Pink Fusion locks that now swept the top of her shoulders. She ignored the wide-eyed stare from a man who drove up beside Todd's car. In this laid-back town, one didn't see many like her; that was for certain.

"Can you help my mommy?" a soft voice said nearby.

Startled, Noelle looked out her window. A small girl of about six stood by the car, her short coat unbuttoned and with nothing covering her mussed blond hair. Several feet behind, a boy of about the same age stood, wearing mittens, a muffler, and a hat with his coat.

"Please, Miss Angel, can you help her?"

Noelle blinked at the woebegone expression on the girl's wind-chapped face. What were these children doing out at this time of night? She pushed at the control to lower the window further.

"Where is your mommy?"

"She's sleeping, but she won't wake up." Tears shone in the child's gray eyes. "Please help her."

Todd rejoined Noelle. The girl abruptly backed up, her expression wary.

"It's all right," Noelle said. "He's a friend of mine. Tell me, sweetie, exactly where is your mommy?"

The child hooked her hand around the boy's mitten. "She's where the ducks live."

"The ducks. You mean at the park?"

The girl nodded, and Noelle quickly filled Todd in on the situation. He set the food down, turned off the ignition, and grabbed the keys from the switch.

"Can you lead me to where she is?" he asked the girl, locking his door and shutting it.

"Will the angel come, too?"

"Angel?"

The little girl pointed to Noelle. "The strawberry angel."

Amusement flickered over Todd's face. "Sure. But we really should go now and see if we can wake your mommy."

Embarrassed, but also feeling a sense of urgency, Noelle got out of the car. They followed the children to the public park located behind the store. The girl glanced over her shoulder twice, as if to make sure they still were there, each time giving Noelle a shy smile.

Near the pond, a minivan sat off the asphalt, hidden behind some bushes. Steam covered the inside of the windows. Todd wrenched open the sliding door. A young woman lay on the seat, twisted up in a blanket, her face shimmering with perspiration.

"Ma'am?" Todd put a hand to her cheek. She didn't stir. "She's burning up. My cell phone's in my jacket. Call 911."

Noelle did so, noticing piles of clothes scattered in the back, two pillows, and a carton containing sparse amounts of boxed food and two oranges. One large suitcase and a small one were stacked near the rear door.

"Where do you kids live?" she asked once she ended the call, already suspecting the answer.

"Nowhere."

The little boy jabbed his elbow into the girl's arm. "Mama

said we're not s'pposed t' tell."

The girl looked at him, her brows drawn together. "It's okay, Scottie," she whispered loudly. "She's the strawberry angel, like in my story. She's going to help us."

At a loss to explain the girl's obvious faith in her and her curiosity piqued by the child's strange comment, Noelle did what she could to reassure the children. Soon, sirens wailed in the distance. In a matter of minutes, policemen and para-medics arrived on the scene. One of the officers, Jack, she recognized as a former high school classmate.

"Noelle, is that you?" He let out a disbelieving whistle as he walked her way. "What did they do to you at Beryl's shop? You look like a costume reject left over from October."

"Wow, thanks, Jack. That's one I haven't heard. But the hair color isn't your sister's doing. It's mine."

In the van's indoor light, she saw him wince. "Sorry. New look from the big city? Never mind. Beryl's always telling me I've got a big mouth. So what's the situation here?" His manner at once became businesslike as he glanced at the paramedics working over the woman. Surprise again lifted his brows. "Todd?"

"Heya, Jack. Yeah, it's me." Todd filled him in on what little they knew while Noelle stood with the children and watched the EMTs strap their mother onto a stretcher. The woman opened her eyes. "Selena?"

"Mommy?" The girl stepped forward, looking uncertain.

Along with her partner, a female paramedic continued to roll the stretcher to the back of a waiting ambulance, all the while assuring the woman that the kids would be well taken care of and she could see them later.

"There's no one for them to stay with." The mother's voice rose to a desperate pitch. "Please don't take me away from them."

"I wanna go with my mommy," Selena cried, rushing forward.

Jack stepped up and put a detaining hand on her shoulder. "You can't ride in the ambulance, little girl. But don't worry. I'll take you and your brother to the hospital so you can be with your mom."

Selena evaded his hand and ran back to Noelle, ducking behind her. She wrapped her arms tightly around Noelle's waist. "I want the angel to take us." The teary words came muffled, spoken into Noelle's coat.

"Angel?" Jack asked, as if he hadn't heard correctly.

"I think she means me," Noelle said, embarrassed. "Todd?"

"I don't have a problem with it, if Jack doesn't. I'm parked at the mini-mart."

Jack appeared more relieved than put out. "Great. You two—er, four—can meet us there. Phil, you ready?" he called to his partner, who was taking down the minivan's license number.

"Can I ride in the back of the police car instead?" the boy piped up.

"No." Selena shot him a frown as she stepped to Noelle's side. She looped a hand around Noelle's wrist and his. "We stick together, like Mommy said."

Lights flashing, the ambulance sped away. The police returned to their car, and Todd and Noelle took the path with the children to the mini-mart.

Once inside Todd's car, Scottie perched on the edge of the backseat, his arms crossed over Noelle's bucket seat. "What's that smell?" he asked, smacking his lips.

Todd exchanged a look with Noelle. She gave a faint nod, and he glanced over his shoulder at Scottie. "Bratwurst sandwich. Want some?"

"Yeah!" In one motion, the boy grabbed the offering and crammed a bite into his mouth. "Thanks," he mumbled around the mouthful of food.

"Would you like one, too?" Noelle asked Selena.

The girl nodded. "Please, thank you." Her words were subdued, and she was more ladylike as she took her first bite. But after that, the sandwich disappeared much more quickly.

During the drive, Noelle glanced at the children, who gobbled down their sandwiches, barely swallowing what was in their mouths before wolfing down another bite. She wondered when they'd last eaten. Judging from their mom's condition, it probably had been too long.

By the time they reached the hospital, both Scottie and Selena sat side by side, sleeping, their heads propped against each other. Traces of mustard smeared the edges of their mouths.

"Oh, aren't they just adorable?" Noelle whispered, a soft look on her face.

"Yeah." Todd studied Noelle.

Selena woke to Noelle's gentle shake, but Scottie snuggled deeper into the vinyl seat. Todd wound up carrying the boy inside, while Selena slipped her hand into Noelle's and walked beside her. The looks Noelle got, with her wild pink hair, light red dress, and white fur coat, ranged from flabbergasted to amused. Some people glanced her way frequently, but pretended not to when they made eye contact. Todd gave Noelle credit for keeping her cool and ignoring the attention.

In the emergency waiting area, the bright lights woke Scottie, and he complained about being thirsty. While Noelle spoke with a nurse, Todd bought two sodas from a machine in the lobby. The kids took them with a polite thank-you but didn't open them.

"Don't you like that kind?" Todd asked.

"Mama doesn't let us have sodas 'cause the sugar makes Scottie jumpy. We drink juice."

"Sorry, I should have asked first." Todd retrieved the unopened cans and set them on the magazine table beside Selena, then found a machine that contained 100 percent orange juice. He bought two. This time both kids eagerly grabbed the bottles, their thank-yous much more enthusiastic.

Noelle joined them, casting a glance at the children who sat out of earshot. "Their mother's being examined. I called Cindy, and she said if the woman's homeless, as I suspect, Haven of Hope will do what they can to help. Only problem, there's no room at the shelter, and I'm not sure what we're going to do about those two if their mom ends up being admitted."

"Has social services been called?"

"I would assume from the police report that they'll be contacted, but I don't know if that's been done yet. Our own social services worker at the shelter is on vacation in Florida."

After a wait that seemed endless, a doctor with irongray hair and glasses came from an adjoining corridor. His mouth twitched when he saw Noelle, and Todd detected her slight groan.

"Well, well, if it isn't Noelle Sanders," the doc said. "What have you gone and done to yourself this time?"

"Hi, Dr. Milton. I didn't know you'd be here tonight. I heard you were on vacation." Her expression was sheepish as she explained to Todd, "Dr. Milton's an old friend of my father's."

"I know Todd," the doctor said. "How's the knee?"

"Kept me off the football field," he joked, though that fact still smarted. He'd held such hopes for a career in professional football.

"Hm, yes." The doctor grew serious. "Are you here about the woman brought in from the park?"

"Yes. How is she? Do you know yet what's wrong with her?"

"Now, Noelle, you know the law won't allow me to divulge such information without her written permission."

"Of course. I wasn't thinking." Her brow furrowed as she looked toward where Selena and Scottie sat. "We brought her children. They're sitting right there." She nodded toward the two chairs a short distance away.

"Ah, yes. She hasn't stopped asking for those two." The doctor cast a fleeting glance at the kids. "Under the circumstances, I'll need to give them a quick checkup. Child Protective Services will be contacted, of course."

"I assumed that." Noelle glanced at the children then

back at the doc. "Any chance I can speak with her? To ask if there's anyone I can call to take the children? We obviously can't leave them here overnight."

"I suppose it's necessary, but keep it brief."

After Dr. Milton gave both Selena and Scottie a clean bill of health, Noelle herded the two into an elevator, with Todd bringing up the rear. Once the foursome reached their mother's floor, however, the children balked at the idea of staying with Todd in the waiting area.

"Please, I want to see my mommy," Selena begged quietly.

"I'm not sure you can this late, sweetie."

"Please?"

Selena's woebegone expression tugged at Noelle's heartstrings. She darted a look at Todd then moved toward the nurse's station to inquire. The nurse appeared relieved.

"That lady's been fretting over her kids since she was brought up here. I'm sure that seeing them will make all of us rest easier, but I'll ask you to keep it short, and keep it quiet. Most all of the patients are sleeping."

Permission given, they headed to the room. Noelle stood sandwiched between both children, who now seemed frightened by all the hospital equipment and seeing their mom in the midst of it. A plump, middle-aged nurse was fiddling with an IV attached to the patient's hand. A closed curtain shielded the other patient, and Jack stood in front of it in his black, intimidating policeman's uniform.

"Are we interrupting?" Noelle asked him.

"Nah, I just have a coupla questions for the lady. It can wait."

"It most certainly should wait, Officer," the nurse said, her tone clipped. "This woman needs rest. You can come back tomorrow to question her." With that, she whisked from the room, almost running into Todd who stood in the hall by the open door.

The woman's wan, pale face crumpled with worry. Shadows darkened the area beneath her eyes. "Who are you?" she asked Noelle, her anxious gaze dropping to Selena who tightly held on to Noelle's hand.

"Don't let the wild pink hair and outfit fool you," Jack cut in. "Noelle's good people; she volunteers at the local women's shelter, and her family and mine go to the same church."

"I'll vouch for everything Jack said," Todd added. "All of us are old friends."

"I'm Noelle Sanders. And you are?"

"Miranda Fitzgerald," the woman croaked. "I—I can't pay for this."

"Let's not worry about that right now," Noelle soothed. "I talked to the director of the local shelter, a friend of mine, and she assured me that they'll help in whatever way they can. And for what they can't do, they'll refer you to those who can."

Dr. Milton strode into the room. "Glad I caught you, Noelle. I was about to head home, when I noticed the little one left this behind." He held out Selena's navy coat. The child took it, a sheepish expression on her face.

"Oh, Selena," her mother said, exasperated. "What've I told you about that, honey? First it was your hat and gloves, now your coat. We can't afford for you to lose that, too."

"I'm sorry, Mama." Tears wobbled in the child's words. She sidled closer to Noelle.

"Well, I should be heading home before the little woman starts to worry," Dr. Milton said with a wink. "Say hi to your dad for me, Noelle. I'm hoping we can take another fishing trip in the spring. As for you," he said as his gaze turned to his patient. "You need rest. I'll be back to check on you tomorrow." He looked at Jack. "A word with you?"

"Sure." Jack seemed disgruntled but headed for the door. The doctor followed him out.

Scottie pulled on Noelle's long skirt, and she bent to hear him. "I hafta go to the bathroom," he whispered loudly enough for all to hear.

"I'll take him," Todd said, reaching for his hand.

"I have to go, too," Selena announced.

"Go with your brother, Selena," their mom said. "I want to talk to Miss Noelle."

"I'll find a nurse to go with Selena," Todd said, looking bamboozled.

Once the two women were alone, Miranda began, "I don't have anyone to take care of the children. Will your shelter take them, at least for tonight or until I can try to make other arrangements?"

"I'm sorry." Noelle wished she had better news. "They're not allowed to take the children without you there, too. Regardless, they're full up right now. I've put your names on a waiting list."

Miranda seemed surprised.

"I've seen enough homeless people to recognize the signs," Noelle gently explained as the woman lowered her head. "It's nothing to be ashamed of, to be without a home. It can happen to anyone."

"After my husband divorced me, I lost my job, then my apartment," Miranda whispered. "Things never got better, so I decided to head to my brother's, hoping he could help us. Then we had car trouble, and so many other things went wrong. . . ." Her words drifted off. "I tried to call him, but the number's been disconnected and I have no idea where he lives, except that it's in the next town—in Fairview. But I've run out of money."

Noelle sympathized with Miranda's plight. "We'll find him." She said the words with assurance, trusting God to give direction as He had so many times in the past. "What about alimony? Don't you receive that?"

"I have no idea where my ex is. He's a trucker, but I don't know who he works for now, since he got fired from his last job. We haven't heard from him in over a year." The woman fidgeted, her fingers plucking at the sheet. "I hate to ask, but will you take Selena and Scottie with you, 'til I can figure out something else?"

Miranda's plea shocked Noelle into silence.

"Please. I've never known Selena to bond so quickly with anyone. She's shy, but she was actually holding your hand. She seems to trust you. And after what that police officer and doctor said, I do, too."

"She thinks I'm an angel," Noelle murmured, still rocked by the woman's request.

Dawning awareness lit Miranda's blue eyes, and the woman smiled for the first time. "Of course. All the more reason I want you to take them. Like I said, I can't pay you, but when I'm outta here, I can clean for you or something. I've only worked retail, but I know how to clean a house."

Her desperation prompted Noelle. "Don't worry about

reimbursing me, Miranda. I'll be glad to have Selena and Scottie stay with me."

After blowing kisses to their mama from the doorway of her room, the children left the hospital with Todd and Noelle. Noelle filled Todd in on Miranda's request, and he was amazed at Noelle's agreement to take on a stranger's kids. She was quite a woman. Then again, he'd never known her to deny anyone with a need.

Once they collected the children's suitcase from the minivan, Todd drove Noelle to her car and they transferred kids and luggage to it. He waved away her good night, fully intending to follow her home. She didn't seem surprised when he pulled up behind her at the duplex.

"They're sound asleep," she whispered, "and I hate to wake them. I'll go clear off my bed, and you can carry them inside."

Todd nodded, reaching for the closest child, Scottie, whose thumb slid from his partially open mouth. Inside the duplex, Noelle motioned Todd to an open door and he carried the boy to a double bed, with sheets and a fluffy blanket pulled back. He collected Selena from the car and laid her beside her brother. Noelle pulled off small shoes and coats and Scottie's hat, muffler, and mittens without waking either of the children, while Todd made a third trip for their suitcase and set it just inside the bedroom door. Noelle covered the kids to their necks with the bedding before she and Todd left the room.

Noelle shut the door with a soft click. "It just occurred to me that you've never had dinner. Would you like a sandwich? Or I've got a couple of frozen dinners I could microwave."

Todd studied her glowing face—no longer glowing pink, but glowing just the same. Any food sounded like manna from heaven right now—even breadsticks. But the hour was late, and for him to be in her apartment during this time of the night—or rather, early morning—might be misconstrued by any night owl neighbors.

"I should get home." He saw disappointment flit into her pretty green eyes, and quickly added, "But we still need to set a time to get together and discuss plans for building the set."

"That's right." She brightened. "Can you come by tomorrow?"

"I'll be here after work."

Chapter 4

Noelle poured steaming coffee into an oversized earthenware mug, savoring the aroma of freshly ground beans. The phone rang. She grabbed it before its persistent chortling could disturb the children, still sleeping, though it was almost noon. "Hello?"

"Miss Sanders?"

"Yes."

"This is Mr. Robison, manager of Cartell's Discount Drugs. I understand you spoke with one of my employees this morning about a misfortune you had regarding a bottle of hair coloring you purchased from our store?"

"Yes, I did." Noelle was still rankled from that call. The woman had made it sound as if Noelle was completely to blame for not noticing the labels on box and bottle were different. Perhaps the woman was partly correct—Noelle should have checked—but the truth was, she'd been too rushed to take notice.

"I overheard the conversation and want to apologize for my employee's discourtesy," the elderly man explained, "as well as to apologize for the incident itself. Two small boys were caught yesterday switching face makeup in boxes. I have no doubt that's what happened with your box, as well. I'm sorry you suffered the brunt of their prank, and to make up for any inconvenience, Cartell's would like to issue you a fifty-dollar gift certificate, redeemable on any item in our store."

She was about to open her mouth and say that wasn't necessary, but a glance toward her closed bedroom door stopped her. "Thank you, Mr. Robison. I'll be in today."

The call she dreaded, the one to her manager, went about as well as Noelle expected.

"What do you mean you can't come in this afternoon?" Rhoda squealed. "Can't you get anyone else to watch those kids? They're not even yours!"

"I know, but I made a promise. I tell you what—you said you needed someone to head those craft classes next month. Give me today off, and possibly tomorrow, and you have your woman."

"That's great. And in the meantime, what am I supposed to do about the wall-to-wall customers and one cashier?"

"How's Darlene working out?"

"Fine. But she's a student and can only work part-time. You know that."

Noelle hesitated. She had no right to offer information before discussing it with the kids' mom first, but she tested the waters anyway. "I might know someone who can help. Only drawback, it would probably be a week or two or more before she could start work." She told her about Miranda Fitzgerald.

"That's one really big drawback, Noelle. The lady has pneumonia, is wired up to a hospital bed—and you think she can be a help to me in what way?" Rhoda's sarcasm came to the fore, a sign that she hadn't gotten her noon coffee break and semisweet chocolate fix.

"I'll see if I can find someone to watch the kids tomorrow," Noelle promised. Though she had no idea who would be available. A door opening behind her and the scuffing of socks on carpet alerted her that the children were awake. "I'll call you later."

"It had better be with good news."

Noelle hung up the phone and turned to face her guests. "Did you two sleep well?"

Selena shrugged. Their clothes from the day before were rumpled, and their golden hair was in snarls. But their eyes were bright, their faces dewy fresh.

"Hungry?" Noelle asked.

Selena tilted her head as if the question posed were a difficult one. "What do angels eat for breakfast?"

"Bet I know," Scottie chirped hopefully. "Cotton candy— 'cause it's like clouds. And 'cause it's pink!"

"No." Noelle chuckled. "Just scrambled eggs, bacon, and muffins with strawberry or grape jam. Sound okay?"

"Yeah!" The kids shot like arrows toward the table and pulled out chairs, scraping them over the tiles.

"I'll bet you eat lots of strawberry stuff 'cause you're the strawberry angel, huh?" Selena asked.

Noelle could no longer contain her curiosity. "Why do you call me that?"

"I'll show you." Selena slid off her seat and raced for the bedroom. Noelle heard her unbuckling the suitcase. Soon she came back with a picture book tucked under one arm. "See," she said, opening to the first page.

Noelle eyed the pink-haired angel in the long, strawberry-colored gown, who hovered amid cottony clouds. The cute, illustrated character was hardly a mirror image, but she understood why the girl might draw comparisons. "I hate to disappoint you, Selena. But I'm as human as you are. I'm certainly no angel."

The child's smile faded and her lips began to tremble as if she might actually cry. Scottie crawled off his chair and tiptoed to stage whisper in his sister's ear. "Maybe she's not s'pposed to say she's an angel. Like in that movie we saw with Kelly."

Selena's face cleared. "Oh—right," she answered just as softly. "She has to be quiet about it, like being a secret agent angel. Her work's top secret."

A secret agent angel? This was really getting out of hand.

The phone rang—either saving her or interrupting her. Noelle wasn't sure how to view the distraction. She snatched up the receiver. "Hello?"

"Everything okay in nursery land?"

Saving her—definitely. Todd's voice layered a ray of warmth to the somewhat dismal morning. "Everything's just peachy keen." She used one of her grandmother's sayings.

"Sure that's not strawberry topped?" he asked lightly.

She rolled her eyes at his weak joke. Would she ever live this hair-color fiasco down?

"Sorry. Couldn't resist. Your voice sounds tight. What gives?"

She explained the situation at work and her need to find a temporary babysitter or risk Rhoda's wrath. "I doubt my manager will fire me. She needs me too badly. But I understand where she's coming from. This close to the holidays, working retail is comparable to managing a zoo."

"Let me see what I can do. I might be able to help."

"You?" Surprise raised Noelle's voice an octave. "What about your job?"

"Not me, no. I'm not up for day care duties. But my sister might be willing. I need to run it by her first. By the way, we still on for tonight?"

"Sure." The matter of building the Christmas set could be arranged by phone, but nothing would entice her to forgo a couple of hours conversing with Todd. Former misunderstandings dealt with, they'd gotten along well last night. "Come by around six."

"I'll bring dinner."

"Thanks. That would be great." Noelle hung up the phone and looked toward her two charges, who were seated quietly, heaping spoonfuls of jam onto bran muffins. With them here, surely any lingering awkwardness between her and Todd would melt away.

Todd raised his knuckles to Noelle's door, but stopped short of knocking when he heard a siren wailing inside. Something loud thumped against the bottom of the door.

"Watch it with that thing, Scottie." Noelle's exasperation was evident in her voice. "You almost knocked it into the table with the lamp."

Todd rapped on the door. Within seconds it swung open. Something whizzed past his hiking shoe, followed by a leaping Scottie, who waved a black control box in his hands.

"See what Miss Noelle got me?" he cried, holding up the remote control to the miniature police car that was racing down the short sidewalk, lights flashing, siren wailing.

"Whoa there, sport." Todd grabbed Scottie's coat sleeve at the shoulder before he could run out into the street. "Does that thing have a stop button?"

Scottie took his hand off the knob. The car came to a standstill. Noelle swung the door wider, her strawberry-pop-vanilla hair tied back in a high ponytail. Selena slid into view under her arm. He took note of Noelle's long blue T-shirt and matching pants—with Selena dressed like an Eskimo beside her.

"Hi again, Mister. See my new mittens. Aren't they pretty?" She shoved two pink-and-purple-clothed hands up toward Todd's face. A hat in a similar color and snowflake pattern snuggled atop her head. "My angel bought them for me when we went to the drugstore, 'cause the man there gave her money 'cause the hair color was wrong."

"Yeah, they're nice." Todd glanced at the mittens, amused to hear the angel reference again. "But isn't it kind of warm inside to wear all that?"

"Oh—I'm *never* taking them off." Selena balled her

mittened hands to her chest as if to guard her treasures.

Todd fully focused on Noelle. "Hi."

"Hi back." She returned his grin.

"Sounds like you've had quite a day."

"Oh, you know how it is. An angel's work is never done. And these two don't come with stop buttons. Their motors are gassed up twenty-four seven."

Todd chuckled and held up a sack. "I brought food."

Scottie reached for the other sack. "French fries?"

"No. Chinese."

Both kids stared at him as if he'd spoken the language. Noelle took the unrolled sack from Scottie's hands.

"Egg rolls, egg foo yung, white rice. . . ." Todd counted off.

"And sweet-and-sour chicken," Noelle ended softly, lifting her gaze from the open bag up to Todd. A wondering look filled her eyes.

"Hope you still like Chinese."

"I haven't had any since our tutoring lessons in high school. This'll be like old times. Did you get it from Ming Lee's Restaurant like we used to?"

"Yeah." Todd couldn't help the goofy grin that came to his face. At least she appreciated his efforts, though he'd clearly struck out with the kids. Scottie had retrieved his toy car and both children disappeared inside the duplex.

"Come on in," Noelle said. "I'll pour us something to drink."

As Todd followed Noelle into a small but tastefully decorated room, his mind wandered down another hallway. Although she worked retail now, he was sure that what his father would view as a setback was only temporary for Noelle. Not so for Todd. After his dream of making it to the NFL died, Todd employed short stints of working at a garage, then a gas station before his most recent position of deliveryman.

Could someone as classy and intelligent as Noelle—forget the accidental pink dye job—be interested in the local deliveryman? Todd knew that a lot of women sought the company of men they could look up to—financially sound and smart, like his dad. If that were the case, Todd didn't stand a chance with Noelle.

Too bad, because he was definitely getting interested in her.

Chapter 5

After giving both kids thick, sloppy peanut butter and jelly sandwiches—the oozing-out-the-bread kind she'd always enjoyed—Noelle rejoined Todd at the table for their Chinese feast. He seemed quiet. Maybe he was just hungry.

"Why'd you quit your job in New York City?" he abruptly asked, his voice sounding a bit strained.

Noelle looked at him, contemplating how to answer. "A year ago I thought I wanted a top position on the team, eventually a partnership, which is where I was heading." She nibbled a forkful of pineapple from her sweet-and-sour chicken and grew thoughtful. "But the company doesn't uphold the values I have. When I finally earned the chance at promotion, I took a step back and looked at where it would lead. I'd had a few spats with my supervisor over too much sex used in selling the products and other moral issues. And I wasn't too happy about some of the clients we had to impress, a beer company to name one. But at the time I thought getting ahead and earning more money were the most important things in life."

"Aren't they?"

She frowned. "You really believe that?"

He was quiet awhile. "No."

"Well, neither do I—now. I eventually realized I was often putting my values on hold to please a client. Being a Christian, I decided I couldn't do that anymore. Bottom line was either I 'stopped being such a prude,' as my former boss put it, or find another place of employment. So I did."

"No regrets?" He fiddled with his milk glass, and she noticed he'd quit eating.

"None. Well, maybe one. I wish I earned as much now as I did two months ago." She made the remark lightly. "But then again money isn't the be-all and end-all of the world. Sure, it helps, but self-respect is more important. And since I quit, I've found I can look myself in the mirror again, even if my freezer isn't stocked with gourmet foods." She blew out a soft laugh. "To sum it all up, I think what's more important than aiming for the highest paying job is to find a job that's a perfect fit, especially when it comes to ethics. I love my volunteer work at the center and being with the kids there. And once the Christmas rush is over I just may find that I love my paying job at the craft store, too." She grinned to show she was kidding again.

Todd slapped his palm to the table. "That reminds me. My sister said she could watch Selena and Scottie tomorrow or whenever you need her, so you can go to work. She has five kids around the same age. They're all staying at my parents' through the holidays."

"Oh, that's great. I should call Miranda and clear it with her, but I can't imagine she'd say no."

"You didn't go to the hospital today, did you?"

Noelle halted her egg roll's progress to her mouth. "How'd you know that?"

"When Selena didn't include it on the list of things you did, I wondered."

"Ah. Well, they did talk to their mom on the phone. Miranda told me she doesn't want the children to see her with all the added equipment around her and get even more upset than they were last night. She asked that I call her room to let the kids talk to her in the morning and at bedtime."

Selena and Scottie approached the table, their plates and glasses empty. Even the crumbs were missing.

"What can we do now?" Scottie asked.

Noelle thought a moment. "How about each of you draw

your mom a picture, and we can mail it to her?"

"Really?" Selena's eyes shone.

"Sure. You'll find colored pencils and markers in that plastic shoe box on the TV stand. Blank paper is in a pile next to it."

The kids scurried away like rabbits excited to find an untouched lettuce patch. Todd and Noelle resumed their conversation and the minutes passed, but she sensed something was still bothering him. Before she could inquire, Scottie and Selena were back.

Noelle eyed them in disbelief. "That was quick."

"We're finished." Selena held up a sheet of paper.

A mother and two children had been drawn next to a decorated house in the snow, with a Christmas tree outside. An angel with pink hair and gown hovered above, holding a star. Noelle felt the blush and glanced at Scottie's picture. A huge turkey—created by the tracing of a small hand—ran from a smiling boy who carried a fork and knife.

Noelle laughed. What different personalities these two had!

"They're both very nice. I'm sure your mom will love them. I'll get stamps tomorrow and mail them first thing," she promised.

"So whatta we do now?" Scottie asked.

"Now?" Noelle was stumped. The clock showed two

hours until what Miranda had said was their bedtime. "You could draw another picture, I suppose."

Neither of the children seemed too thrilled with that idea.

"Let me see what I can think up." Noelle took the empty plates and glasses to the kitchen sink. The small funnel she'd used to make orange juice that morning sat nearby. Staring at it, she felt an idea begin to gel.

She spun around with a smile, palms going to the counter on either side of her, and faced the trio who looked at her expectantly.

"How about we make a craft? A Christmas angel."

Selena squealed. "Yeah!"

Noelle was already sliding open the drawer with the various sized plastic funnels, glad she'd bought a set of them. She dug out the largest. "We'll use this for the body, and I have some craft items in a box in my closet. The big brown one labeled 'art supplies.' Todd, do you mind getting it?"

"Not a bit." He set to his task, while Noelle cleared off the table and gathered other things they might need.

"Scottie, will you bring that box of pencils and markers over here, please? Let's see, what else. . ." She stood back, one arm across her waist, her other hand at her chin. Thumb propped beneath, she tapped her forefinger against her lower lip. Surveying the small cache of treasures slowly building on the table as Scottie set the shoe box down, she counted off items. "Scissors, glue, scraps of material—"

"Pink hair," Selena intoned.

Full attention snagged, Noelle stopped her finger tapping. "What?"

"The angel's got to have pink hair—like you." Selena's smile was wide. "It's got to be special."

Feeling the usual dreaded warmth rise to her face, Noelle turned again to study the items on the table. "I'm not sure I have anything pink that would work, Selena." She looked toward the hall closet that held her sewing kit. "But I do have some red tassels I bought on clearance. I thought I might make a belt, but never did."

Todd returned with the box and dropped it on the table. "You really love your sales, don't you?"

"Yeah." Noelle let out a half laugh riddled with embarrassment. "You'd think I would learn by now that clearance isn't always the best way to go."

"That how you got the hair?"

She nodded.

A tender smile tipped his mouth. "Oh, I don't know. Sometimes these things work out for the best."

Noelle eyed him as if he now possessed her pink hair. He walked closer.

"If not for your new dye job"— he lowered his voice for

her ears only— "those two might still be living in a van, with their mom in need of a doctor's care. Selena thought you were—what was it she called you? Oh, yeah. The strawberry angel." He grinned. "That's the only reason she approached you for help."

Selena stopped sorting through a box and looked at them, then scurried to grab her picture book from the couch. She opened to the first page and shoved it at Todd. "See, there she is."

Todd's eyebrows lifted as he drew the book closer. "Wow." His eyes shone with amusement as he glanced at Noelle. "That's uncanny. Pink hair, long dress, and everything."

"Yeah, uncanny." Noelle set to work tearing off the safety plastic from a new bottle of glue. Now that she thought about it, the whole incident was just that. Uncanny. Or maybe God-driven was a better description. Todd was right. Selena probably wouldn't have approached her last night if her hair hadn't been pink and she hadn't been wearing a long gown close to the same color. Not if she was as shy as her mom said. A rapid surge of gratitude showered through Noelle at how awesome God was to bring some good out of her hair-dying catastrophe.

"When are we gonna make this thing?" Scottie asked, sorting through the odds and ends in the box.

Noelle smiled at him. "Right now."

They each pulled out a chair from the table, and soon Noelle was directing them in the necessary steps to make their own, one-of-a-kind, strawberry angel.

Todd had no idea what he was doing. Carpentry work he could manage. Painting the background of a stage set a solid color should be easy work, too. But cutting circles from material and affixing all sorts of minuscule shiny doodads to the cloth-encased funnel was out of his element. So was drawing a face with a fine-point marker on the scrap of material tied around a Styrofoam ball for a head. After three failed attempts, Noelle took over that chore. Good thing there appeared to be a lot of light-colored material in the scraps bag.

The kids were definitely enjoying themselves. Todd watched Noelle show Scottie how to make the halo from tinsel and Selena the wings from feathers, noticing how relaxed she seemed around the kids. She really liked them, and vice versa. To Selena, Noelle's word was law, and Todd had noticed how the child seemed to shed some of her shyness only when Noelle reassured her that Todd was a friend.

Feeling left out, but not minding so much because the hot, spiced apple cider Noelle had put on the stove was calling to him, Todd rose from his chair.

Noelle looked up. "Where do you think you're going?"

"To dish out some cider?" he asked hopefully.

"Nope. Back to work. You get the final job of hot-gluing the items onto the funnel. I don't think the craft glue will hold the wings on well, and the head could use some help, too."

She handed over the body of the angel, along with its flimsy wings, into Todd's large hand. He held the objects awkwardly, afraid he would crush them. The excess material covering the head had been tucked through the narrow tubing, but the smiling face flopped to one side.

"Slave driver," he teased. Noelle was even bossier than when she'd tutored him in high school, but Todd didn't mind so much. Not if it brought that smile to her face.

"You haven't been doing anything for the past ten minutes," she countered in mock indignation. Her eyes twinkled, while her mouth pouted just a bit—and sparkled, too.

Sitting back down, he reached over to brush gold glitter from her jaw, discovering her skin felt silky smooth to the touch. She jumped a bit, as if shocked.

He showed her the metallic flecks on his finger. "You had some glitter there."

She raised her hand to swipe at the area near her mouth, though the glitter was now gone. "Thanks."

Several seconds elapsed before she looked at him again. "I'll get us some cider while you finish the angel." Noelle headed for the cupboard and began pulling out ceramic mugs. She ladled steaming cider into four of them. The strawberry ponytail swung in time to her actions.

Why hadn't he ever asked her out their senior year? Sure, he'd gone steady with Diane, a girl from the pep squad, for two semesters, but after his accident on the field there'd been a stretch when he hadn't dated much at all. Diane had broken up with him after he'd left the team.

He continued to watch Noelle, appreciating the lines of her slender form and her bubbly efficiency. Truth was, he'd been attracted to her in high school, but he'd been so sure she wouldn't want to go out with someone who was a dunce to her Einstein. Her GPA had been in the top scores, and Todd's. . . Well, he'd graduated from high school anyway.

"Finished?" she asked as she turned, holding two mugs.

"Not yet." Todd picked up the hot glue gun and began attaching items. She set his mug down on a cleared spot of the table.

"You are allowed to take a break," she said, amused, obviously not noticing that he hadn't begun. "I'm really not a slave driver anymore, like I was when I coached you in English Lit."

He finished what was expected of him before taking his

first sip. The cinnamon-apple taste warmed his insides but didn't fill the strange emptiness that had crept in unawares. The children, warned not to touch the angel until it dried, scampered off to watch what was left of a Christmas TV special.

"Why'd you come back to Hartford Falls after you quit your job?" Todd posed the question he'd wanted to ask since day one.

At his abrupt words, Noelle looked up from taking a sip of her cider. He smiled to lessen any unintended sting. "You didn't have to leave New York City. You could have found another job there."

"I suppose." She stared at the mess on the table and took another sip before explaining. "When I went to New York City, I was looking for something. I thought I would find it there. But when I stopped allowing other people's expectations to squelch my own beliefs, my goals changed, and I realized that what I really wanted was here at home all the time."

"And what's that?"

"Miss Noelle!" Selena suddenly screeched. "Tell Scottie to give me the remote."

"I had it first!"

Noelle glanced at the silver and black Art Deco wall clock. "Sorry, kids. Bedtime. Selena, you're first in the bath tonight. Scottie, you can help me clean up. Then we'll call your mom."

"Is the angel dry yet?" The girl ran to the table and reclaimed her chair, kneeling on the seat.

"No, not yet."

Propping her elbows on the table and her chin in her fists, Selena smiled and studied the angel. "It's so pretty. Can we give it to someone for Christmas?" she asked hopefully.

"I think that's a lovely idea. Who do you want it to go to? Your mom?"

Selena shook her head. "I want it for my babysitter when we lived in Sche-ned-aky."

"Schenectady?" Noelle clarified.

"Uh-huh. She once had black hair with a pink stripe in it. And she likes angels. She's got a really pretty shirt that's got an angel on it. It glows in lots of shiny colors."

"But, Selena," Scottie said, coming up to the table. "Kelly went away, 'member?"

Selena sobered. "Oh, yeah. Her dad sent her to charm school. What's charm school?"

"A place where they help young girls behave like ladies," Noelle said as she replaced the items in the box.

"If you remember the name of the school, I might be able to help," Todd cut in. "I have a global tracking device I use at work that can find just about anybody."

"Even our uncle?" Scottie asked, eyes big.

"Your uncle?" Todd cast a curious glance Noelle's way.

"Didn't I tell you?" Noelle slapped a hand to her forehead. "I didn't tell you. So much has been going on." She explained why Miranda and the children had been living in a van.

"It'll be difficult to find him without an address, but I'll see what I can do. You'd be surprised how easy it is to track someone and get information about them, even on the Internet." He grabbed his jacket from the chair back where it was draped. "I'd better get out of here and let you get these two to bed."

"But we never discussed the Christmas set or what time you could come build it."

Todd's movements slowed as he slipped into his jacket. "No, we didn't, did we? Tell you what, I can probably get Saturday morning and afternoon off if that'll work for you."

"I'll make it work." Noelle walked with him to the door and opened it, revealing how dark the sky had gotten. A light, wet snow was falling. "Thanks for the Chinese."

Her beautiful green eyes seemed to say more. So much more. . . He wanted to kiss her. He couldn't remember ever wanting anything so badly.

"Miss Noelle?" Selena called from a back room. "Can you run the water so my bath won't be hot?"

Todd zipped up his jacket. "I'd better let you go. I'll see you this Saturday. Around ten in the morning okay?"

"Sounds perfect."

With the added coziness of her smile to warm him, Todd headed for his car. But the niggling fact that she was, as his father would say, "out of his league" soon stole even that bit of warmth away.

Chapter 6

Saturday dawned, freezing but clear, and Noelle quickly herded the kids into her car and drove to the shelter. Once home to the Mackenzie family, built at the turn of the twentieth century, and tucked at the edge of a small wood with a glimpse of the Catskill Mountains beyond, Haven of Hope now belonged to many women and their children in need of a temporary place to stay. The homeless, the battered, the destitute found their way to the sprawling white Georgian to seek comfort, counsel, and aid. Reconstructed to fit the ministry's needs, Haven of Hope had proven a refuge to many, a springboard to help them start new lives. Noelle loved being part of such a ministry and was excited that they'd received enough donations to start building another wing. Presently, they could house thirty, besides the live-in staff, but Cindy hoped to double that amount next year.

The kids crowded close to Noelle as she walked up the circular drive. She felt sorry for the two. Todd hadn't been able to track down the uncle with only a name to go by, and after seeking a telephone operator's help, Noelle discovered that the man had no listing. All they knew about Jimmy Stravinski was that he was a freelance journalist who'd recently moved.

Inside, Cindy greeted them, looking as fresh and elegant, as always, in a soft-yellow and cream-colored sweater and slacks. With a friendly smile she introduced herself to the children then asked Beth, a young staff member, to take them to the playroom.

Selena grabbed Noelle's hand, adhering to her side like Velcro. "No thank you. I want to stay with Miss Noelle."

Beth bent down and laid a gentle hand on her shoulder. "Wouldn't you like to see all the neat toys we have? There's a few kids in the playroom right now."

"No." Selena pressed her face into Noelle's coat. Noelle could actually feel her shaking.

"I'll take her," Noelle said.

Both Cindy and Beth nodded with understanding smiles. They were accustomed to dealing with fearful children who didn't want to be touched or talked to, so Selena's behavior wasn't at all unusual.

"Can I bring my new police car?" Scottie asked, as exuberant as ever, holding up his toy for their inspection.

"Sure," Beth said. "Show me how it works?"

Once inside the cheery playroom, Scottie immediately headed for a round table where two kids were working with plastic building blocks. Both lost interest in the colored squares when they saw Scottie's car, and he gave them a demonstration. Selena walked inside but hung back against the mint-and-ivory wallpaper, as if hoping to become one of the stripes in the pattern. She gripped Noelle's hand in a death clutch.

Beth bent down to talk to another girl, Skylar, who moved away from playing with a miniature play kitchen and approached Selena. The girl with the beautifully slanted Asian eyes and straight dark hair was two years older than Selena and invited her to play. At first Selena wouldn't budge, but after a few minutes, when Skylar had gone back to pretend-cooking with her plastic dishes, Selena let go of Noelle's hand and crept forward. Only when the child was caught up in baking a cake, per Skylar's instructions, to feed three dolls seated at a play table, did Noelle move silently away, confident that Selena would be all right for the next couple of hours.

Following the bangs of a hammer to what was once a ballroom, she found Todd busy at work. Impressed with the progress he'd made, Noelle voiced an approving, "Wow."

"Oh, hey, I didn't hear you come in." Todd's hammer

paused mid bang. A lock of dark hair lay against his forehead, and Noelle fought the urge to reach out and let it curl around her finger. Muscular arms were clearly defined beneath the short sleeves of his blue T-shirt, and she imagined how good it would feel to be wrapped in their protective embrace.

To cover her embarrassment at her runaway thought—and glad Todd couldn't read her mind—she rotated in a half circle, surveying the set in progress in the middle of the high-ceilinged room. "I would have gotten here earlier, but it wasn't easy getting the kids out of the house this morning. It's amazing how many things were missing when it was time to go—shoes, socks, Selena's mittens, Scottie's coat." Grinning, she tucked her hands in her sweater pockets. "Anything I can do to help?"

"Not sure about now. But when it comes time to decorate the backdrop, definitely ask me again."

"I can hold something for you if you need me to, or play gofer. I'm not scheduled to practice scenes with the kids until after lunch, so I'm free 'til then."

"In that case, I'd welcome your company."

For the smile he gave, she would do anything—pound a thousand nails, saw a thousand boards, paint a thousand backdrops. . .

One half of a stable later, she wasn't so sure. She'd accidentally kicked over the container of nails, then almost gave

Todd a black eye when she unknowingly set a heavy can of paint on the end of a wide plank balanced on a metal trash can, just as he bent over, and the board ricocheted upward like a seesaw. Turning now to survey the result of their hard work, she saw that the seven-foot wooden panel they'd just erected was tottering in a slow-motion sway toward them.

"Todd!" she screeched, hurrying to plant her palms against the sheet of wood and try to prevent its downfall. She felt Todd's warmth directly behind as he smacked his hands even higher—causing the panel to catapult in the other direction. Noelle yelped as gravity forced Todd forward—into her—and they both lost their balance. The board slammed to the floor, and they crashed on top of it.

After a couple of stunned, frozen seconds, Todd crawled off Noelle. She felt his hand cover her shoulder. "You okay?"

"I think so." With his help, she sat up—and grew lost in his rich, chocolate-brown irises, now only inches from hers.

He gazed into her eyes intently for several mind-numbing seconds then lowered his focus to her lips. She did the same, noticing again how well shaped his mouth was. His lips were full but masculine. Entirely kissable.

He moved a breath's pace toward her. She barely tilted her head. The approaching sound of children giggling down the hallway grew louder.

Todd jerked back, his gaze flying to hers. "Guess I didn't

use enough nails." His words came out strained.

"Guess not."

Another tense heartbeat passed, as if he were trying to make a decision, before he stood and helped her from the floor. Two of the older children came running inside.

"Miss Noelle, Miss Cindy wants to talk with you about the play."

"Okay, Nancy. Thanks." Noelle still felt shaky—and disappointed—about the kiss that didn't happen. Would Todd really have kissed her? They were rebuilding their friendship, yes, but could he ever be romantically interested in a ditzy female with Pink Fusion hair and a propensity for making mistakes?

Somehow she doubted it—not after remembering the gorgeous and totally together girls Todd dated in high school.

After eating lunch with the staff, Todd walked with Noelle and somehow found himself in the room where she was to teach the children.

"Noelle," Beth said as she popped into the doorway. "Cindy needs to talk with you again—pronto." With that she was gone.

Noelle turned to Todd. "I should only be a minute. Watch

things for me?" Before he could answer, she was gone, too.

Now what?

"Hiya, guys." He surveyed the eleven children gathered in the small room, which felt smaller with every passing second.

Scottie and Selena were the only ones to smile back. Some of the kids eyed Todd curiously, others with mistrust, but no one answered his greeting. Judging from what he'd heard of the situations and homes some of these children had come from, he couldn't blame them for not trusting a stranger. But he'd been in worse fixes—when crouched in starting position before a football play and staring at the offensive tackle who easily weighed a hundred pounds more than him. So why was he starting to sweat?

A surly-faced boy bounced a grapefruit-sized ball against a wall, catching it and repeating the process in rapid-fire bangs. "Stop it, Jeremy," a girl ordered and pushed him.

"Make me." He pushed her back.

This could get ugly.

Spotting two more rubber balls, Todd scooped them up as an idea struck. "Loan me yours for a minute?" he asked Jeremy.

The boy crossed his arms. "Why should I?"

"Because it's hard to juggle with two."

"Juggle?" a small boy with buckteeth asked. "Like a clown?"

"Yep." Todd began tossing the two balls in the air, in a lozenge-shaped loop, thankful his uncle had taught him years ago, insisting it would help him with his football skills—both to keep his eye on the ball and to catch it.

"Anyone can do that," Jeremy jeered.

"Bet you can't," another boy challenged.

"Bet he can't do it with three," Jeremy shot back.

"Try me," Todd said, keeping his eye on the balls that he kept in constant motion.

The unexpected action of Jeremy lifting his arm in a curve snagged Todd's attention and he lost his timing. Jeremy threw the ball at him—hard. As the other two balls bounced to the floor, Todd took a step back, instinctively putting out a hand to catch the third ball. Stumbling over a chair, balance gone—he fell into it. He missed the third ball, which sailed into the wall behind him, then bounced and rolled past his hiking shoe to land inches away.

The kids laughed, as if watching an old slapstick movie.

Todd grinned. *So, they wanted a clown.*

Amazed to hear peals of children's laughter, Noelle approached the recreational room where she'd left Todd with the kids. Upon entering, she stopped, her mouth dropping open then forming a slow grin.

Todd juggled three balls and missed one—which bounced off his head. The kids laughed again, as he scratched the top of it and pretended to be unable to find the ball that was in plain sight. Two of the smaller children pointed to the blue ball two feet from Todd with giggling shrieks of, "There it is! There!"

Noelle crossed her arms and casually leaned against the doorjamb. She watched his antics until Todd noticed her and lifted his hand in acknowledgment. "Your teacher's back," he told the kids.

"She's not our teacher," one small fry Noelle recognized as Luke said. "She's just supposed to help us learn some stupid play."

"I don't think it's stupid," Todd defended. "The Christmas story is interesting. An adventure. Can you imagine being born in a barn with lambs and goats and cows all around? And kings coming to visit you, bringing treasure?"

"Will you stay and watch?" Scottie asked, and a few other kids joined in with the plea.

"Yes, Todd," Noelle said good-naturedly, uncrossing her arms and walking to the front to join him. "Do stay. I'd love your help. My assistant just called in sick."

"Well, I don't know. . ."

Noelle almost felt sorry for him. She shouldn't have put

him in such a spot. Before she could dig him a way out, he shrugged and smiled. "Maybe for just a few minutes."

Just a few minutes turned into more than an hour. While she prompted and instructed those kids with lines, Noelle was thankful for Todd's presence, which made the older boys less prone to act up. Wanting the children to get acquainted with where they were to stand on the stage in progress, Noelle had arranged for a laundry basket to substitute as a manger and a few chairs to stand in for palm trees.

She watched as three-year-old Ginny abandoned her job as shepherdess, walked to the basket, and crawled atop the bunched blanket inside. Popping her thumb into her mouth, she cuddled the doll that would be baby Jesus close to her heart and closed her eyes.

Todd looked at Noelle in confusion. "Her doll?"

"No. She does that when she gets tired," Noelle explained. "Finds a corner to sleep. Once we found her in the laundry hamper, another time she chose a baby crib." She grinned and glanced at her watch. "All right, that's enough for today."

"What about the craft we're s'pposed to make?" Luke asked. "The presents for our moms? Are we gonna do that next?"

"I don't have all the materials yet. I'll pick them up at work Monday, and we'll do the craft next week."

"Can we make another angel?" Selena whispered. She'd

been quiet for most of the afternoon and Noelle was glad to see her begin to participate, even if it was just to ask a question.

"We could."

"A strawberry one? Like the one we made to look like you?"

"Maybe." The expected heat rose to Noelle's cheeks.

"What do you mean?" a boy named Trevor asked, but Selena clammed up and dropped her gaze to her feet. Instead, Scottie explained the whole thing.

Jeremy gawked at Noelle. "I was wonderin' why you did that to your hair. It's never gonna come out, ya know. My cousin colored hers—made it real dark pink—and even though the beauty place bleached it and stuff, it didn't go away. She even tried to dye it brown, and it ended up lookin' like a purple Tootsie Pop that had been licked a whole bunch."

A tidbit of information Noelle didn't need to hear.

Jeremy headed for the door, then turned and walked backward. "I know—you can be the purple Toostie Pop Angel! Suckers is better than strawberries, anyways." He laughed and raced out the door. A few other children followed him.

Todd looked at Noelle, his eyes sympathetic. "Are you planning on keeping it that way through Christmas?"

"I don't see that I have much choice with both hair salons in town booked. And I'm certainly not going to try to dye it back myself. After what Jeremy said, I'm not sure I'll try at all."

Todd captured a pink strand that lay over the shoulder of her ivory sweater and held it between his fingers. "It is pretty. Christmas-like."

Noelle wrinkled her nose at him, and he laughed.

"Seriously speaking. The color grows on you. I'm beginning to like it."

Noelle wasn't sure if he was teasing or not, but by the serious look that suddenly entered his eyes, she wished they were alone. If four of the children hadn't been present—one trying to juggle balls while the others watched—he might have even kissed her.

Chapter 7

"Sing we now of Christmas, Noel sing we here. . ."

Selena's hand in hers, Noelle walked up the sidewalk with a group from the center—four staff and a few mothers with their children—as they sang their short rendition of an old French carol. They gathered in a semicircle in front of a decorated two-story house, only one of many homes on Cindy's caroling list of those who'd contributed to the shelter. The porch light flicked on, bathing the area in a golden glow, and she nodded to the children to ring their wrist bells.

"Noel, noel, noel, no-ellll. . ." The exuberant words died on her lips once the door swung open.

"Sing we here, no-ellll," the chorus of angelic voices lifted around her while she went mute.

Positioned in the doorway, Todd smiled at Noelle from where he stood behind his mother, who beamed at the carolers. "Oh, how lovely," the dark-haired woman enthused. "Please, do continue."

The group sprang into a rousing stanza of "Dashing through the snow," but Noelle's mind accelerated on a careening course all its own. When had Todd's family moved? She didn't remember them living in this neighborhood, and she certainly hadn't known Todd would be here tonight. Todd's sister had picked up the children from Noelle's apartment every workday, so Noelle never visited their home. Tonight, Cindy was the bearer of the list and drove the van to each residence, so Noelle had been clueless about where they were going.

After a few more songs, ending with "Away in a Manger," the group concluded their performance. Mrs. Brentley invited them inside for hot cocoa, but Cindy politely declined, explaining that the last house on their list—Cindy's mom's—had hot apple cider and hot chocolate waiting. Mrs. Brentley insisted they have something and passed out candy canes.

Scottie ran up to Todd. "Will you come with us?"

"Yeah!" two of the other children chimed in. "Come with us."

"I don't know. Can you use a tenor?" Todd asked Noelle.

Giddiness tickled Noelle that Todd would consider joining them. She could only nod, since her tongue seemed to have thickened. But Cindy piped right up, "Sure! The more the merrier. There's room in the van for another caroler. Your mother, too, if she'd like to come."

"No thanks. I think I'll just stay inside where it's nice and warm. You go on and have a nice time." Briskly rubbing her arms over her knit sweater, Mrs. Brentley smiled at Todd, then Noelle, a twinkle in her eye.

Hmm. Another matchmaker? Noelle wouldn't put it past both their mothers to attempt pairing them off, since Noelle knew the women had become fast friends through their work on the committee. Sure, Noelle would enjoy dating Todd. But she doubted Todd would welcome their moms manipulating things.

As the group continued their amateur concert tour, a talcum-fine snow began to blow, adding to the chill. Yet Noelle felt toasty warm as Todd stayed close. When he casually slipped his arm around her jacket while they caroled in front of the mayor's home, her mind went blank. She sought for the next words to the chorus but couldn't remember them. Afraid to even breathe lest he move his arm away, she stood as still as the snowman on the wide lawn.

Todd felt Noelle stiffen, and cast a sideways glance in her

direction. "Frozen" best described her expression. She didn't seem upset, exactly, rather stunned. Resigned, he lowered his arm from around her shoulders, thinking maybe she was one of those that preferred her own personal space. He didn't want to crowd her, though he missed the feel of her snug beside him.

After visiting a string of other houses, Cindy drove to a retirement center, where they were welcomed with big smiles from those in the recreation room. Two residents sat in wheelchairs while the others sat in high-backed chairs edging the round tables, all of them waiting for the performance to begin.

The carolers sang their tunes, and a number of residents joined in. Afterward, they smiled and conversed with the children. They appeared genuinely happy and grateful for the gift the carolers brought them—the gift of their time and voices. And the children seemed to sense that. It was amazing to see even a troublemaker like Jeremy enter into excited conversation about ice fishing with one of the residents.

"That's sure a pretty dress you have on," a white-haired gentleman who'd introduced himself as Ben said to Selena. He reminded Todd of Barnaby Jones from the TV show reruns, with his hound-dog face, ready smile, and bushy white eyebrows. He even had the Southern drawl.

"Thank you." Clutching her shiny green skirt, Selena

inched closer to Noelle. "My angel got it for me."

Ben's shaggy brows sailed high. "Really? Well, that's down-right interesting. I do believe God gives every one of us an angel to help keep us in line." He cast a glance upward to Noelle, amusement on his features. "And this one's yours, huh?"

Selena nodded, loosening up a bit. "She found us in the park and took care of us. So did he." She pointed to Todd.

"We was tryin' to find our uncle," Scottie jumped in to explain. "He moved away but we don't know where."

"Is that right?"

"Uh-huh. He's a jour—jour—he writes a paper."

"You don't say? And does this paper writer have a name?"

"Uh-huh. His name's Jimmy Stra-vin-si. We couldn't remember his last name 'til Miss Noelle called Mommy at the hospital. She got sick."

Ben's carefree manner disappeared. "You mean Stravinski?"

Scottie nodded. "Yeah. It's hard to say."

Ben directed his attention toward Noelle. "We had a young man come here weeks ago to write a piece on the center. I seem to remember Stravinski was his name. I was one of them he interviewed. You might check at the desk before you leave. They should be able to get in touch with him and find out if he's your man."

"I will." A light shone in Noelle's eyes as she exchanged

glances with Todd. He also hoped this would be the key to finding the uncle.

The fun evening ended at Cindy's mom's house with hot beverages and homemade goodies the older woman passed around. The phone rang and Todd watched Cindy grab it.

"It's been a good night," Todd said to Noelle as she sipped her cider.

"Yes, it has. I'm glad you joined us."

Todd raised his brows. "Really?"

"Yes. The children like you, and that doesn't happen with everyone."

"Only the children?"

A blush colored her face. "Yes, well, I've enjoyed working with you, too. It's been great so far. Like old times, but new ones, too." Quickly, she took a bite of her chocolate chip cookie. Before Todd could probe further, Cindy joined them, her expression grim.

"That was the center," she explained. "Doc Milton called. The kids' mom had a bad reaction to some new medicine. He didn't go deeply into it, but it doesn't look good."

Both Todd and Noelle glanced across the room at the two kids who sat beside each other on the sofa. As though somehow attuned to the situation, Selena set her paper cup down and hesitantly walked their way. "Did I do something wrong?"

"Of course not sweetie." Noelle bent to hug the little girl close. "We just need to pray for your mommy. Because God's bigger than any problem that comes against her or you or anyone. Always remember that. Okay?"

Eyes wide, the child nodded, and they all clasped hands.

Chapter 8

The week before the Christmas play, Noelle and Todd finished details to the set. He'd already spray painted the backdrop midnight blue, and now they both added white dot stars to the surface with small paintbrushes.

"How's the kids' mom?" Todd asked.

"Better now that they've switched medications, but her system is still fighting something. They're running tests."

"Think there's any way she'll be out by Christmas?"

"The doctor says there's always a chance. Each day has brought a little more progress."

"That's good. It must be hard on those two not being able to see her."

"Yes, but Miranda wanted it that way. At least both

Selena and Scottie like staying with me, and I don't mind at all. They're well-behaved kids." Noelle stepped back and surveyed her work. "Think I should put more stars in that corner? We want it to look real."

"It's fine."

"Are you sure?" Noelle tilted her head. The scene seemed off balance.

"You know what your problem is?" Todd approached, his voice teasing. "You're too much the perfectionist."

"Am not."

"Are so."

"Right." Enjoying their banter, she flipped her hair. "That would explain this lovely masterpiece."

Todd chuckled. "Didn't you tell me you colored it because you didn't like the way it was and you wanted it to match your outfit? That reeks of perfectionism to me. And this isn't the first time you've changed your looks either. I seem to recall in our senior year, before Christmas break, you got a perm."

"You remember that?" Uncomfortable prickles reminded her of her attempt at a home perm, which had made her look as if she'd stood outside holding a lightning rod during a thunderstorm. Wanting to forget that little catastrophe, she returned her attention to painting. "I always try a dose of self-improvement around the holidays. Sort of a birthday present to myself, I guess."

"I like you the way you are."

Noelle's brush stopped short of the backdrop. Had she heard him right?

She darted a look his way, but he'd returned to painting stars above Bethlehem's hills.

"So when is your birthday?" he asked.

"Christmas Eve."

"You're kidding. The night of the play? That doesn't seem like much of a birthday for you. You should have someone treating you to a steak dinner at some classy restaurant."

"Oh, I don't mind. I'll be with those I love and that's what's important. The kids, Cindy, Mom, Dad. . ." *And you'll be there*, she silently added.

She wrinkled her nose, critically eyeing her work. "I totally got this off balance. It looks like a major galactic explosion in that corner, but like several lonely stars lost their way over there."

"Perfectionist," he teased.

"Hey!" She grinned. Before she thought about it, she dabbed his wrist with her paintbrush.

"Oh, yeah?" He repaid the favor to her hand.

"No fair!" She laughed. "Your dot is bigger than mine!"

Knowing the paint was nontoxic and could easily be washed off with soap, she dabbed his chin. "You look nice with a white goatee." She giggled.

His eyebrows sailed up and his mouth dropped open as if he couldn't believe what she'd done. Then he dabbed her on the nose.

"Todd," she giggled again, wiping the paint away. "Not on the face. Pink hair is bad enough."

"What's the old saying? All's fair in love and war." His low words teased as he dabbed her cheek, then the other one.

"Todd—stop it!" Laughing, she stepped up close, grabbing his wrist to prevent him from adding another white freckle.

The mood changed between them as swiftly as if someone had flipped a switch, and they stood as still as stage props. His gaze locked with hers.

"Todd?" she whispered after an endless moment, her heart beating faster in anticipation.

The intrusion of his spoken name seemed to decide him. He released her wrist and stepped back, wiping the smear from his chin with one hand. "I should get cleaned up and call it a night. I'll see you at dress rehearsal next Saturday." His easy words didn't match his stiff smile or abrupt movements.

"Okay." Disappointed, she watched him prop his paintbrush in the water can and walk away. What had happened?

At the door, he stopped. Hesitated. Turned.

Before she could think to ask what was wrong, he rapidly bridged the ten feet that distanced them, pulled her into his arms, and firmly kissed her.

Noelle's paintbrush hit the floor.

Her heart still thudded in her ears when he pulled back. "I'd say I'm sorry," he said, his voice low. "But I'm not."

Still mesmerized by his heart-melting kiss and the warmth now simmering in his eyes, she shook her head. "I've wanted you to do that forever," she whispered. "Since senior year, if you want the truth."

With the tips of his fingers, he brushed her hair behind her ear. "I must have been blind then, Noelle. But I've got my eyes wide open now. And I like what I see."

"Even if it's strawberry-topped?"

"Yeah, even then." He smiled.

Their gazes mingled another few seconds before he once more dipped his head. This time his lips settled tenderly, exquisitely over hers. She pressed close to him, wrapping her arms about his neck.

Her fairy tale had come true. The pink angel/princess had won the heart of the dashing messenger/knight.

If only fairy tales could last forever.

The sound of someone clearing her throat returned Noelle to the real world with a jolt, though she felt dazed, as if she'd been abruptly awakened from a dream. She broke away from the wonder of Todd's lips to see Cindy at the door. Todd turned to look, too, keeping his arm loosely wrapped around Noelle's waist.

"Well, it's about time," Cindy said, always to the point, her smile wide. "Sorry to interrupt, but I just came to tell you the news. That tip Ben gave you paid off. We found the kids' uncle."

"That's great!" Noelle exclaimed.

"He just called the center and will be driving here as soon as he can take off from work. He was shocked to hear about Miranda. Since he's temporarily living with a buddy right now—by the way, that's why we couldn't find him—he can't have her move in with him at the apartment. He doesn't make much at his new job yet, but he promised he'd help in whatever way he could."

"Miranda will be so relieved to hear that," Noelle said. "My manager agreed to interview her for a job at the craft store when she's recovered, but I know she's been worried about hospital bills piling up."

"And I have more good news." Cindy fairly beamed. "I called the hospital right after I got off the phone with Jimmy. Miranda's condition has improved—almost a full turnaround. The doctor and staff are amazed."

"That's wonderful! The kids will be thrilled."

"Do you want to tell them or should I?"

"I'd like to. Todd?" Confused, Noelle looked at Todd, who'd just dropped his arm from around her waist. "Want to come along?"

A serious expression replaced his soft-focused one of earlier. "I'll leave that to you, Noelle. I should run a few errands before calling it a night."

"Okay." She tried for a smile but it fell short.

"Bye, ladies. See you at dress rehearsal." With a short wave, he was out the door.

"Don't look so worried," Cindy soothed. "The man's crazy about you. He probably just realized how late it is and that he had other plans, like he said."

"Yeah. Probably." But Noelle's smile felt fake.

Somehow she didn't think that was Todd's only excuse.

"Oh, don't be so nervous," Noelle's mom said, fluffing Noelle's hair over her shoulders. "You'll do fine."

Noelle gave her mother as warm a smile as she could muster. But inside her stomach, caterpillars rapidly metamorphosed into monster butterflies.

Only five minutes until curtain time. For the sake of the play—and the kids—she'd sacrificed any remnant of pride left over from her hair coloring fiasco, donned the Barbie-style gown Cindy had scrounged up at the last minute, and would now take eight-year-old Gwen's place as the Christmas angel.

Yesterday, Gwen's mom decided to take Gwen and visit their estranged family for the holidays. Grateful that the mom was finally willing to mend relationships with her parents, neither Cindy nor Noelle had the heart to ask her to stay one extra day for the play. The bus trip to her hometown would take a day and a half, and they didn't want Gwen's mom to change her mind and chicken out at the last minute. So, thanks to Selena's enthusiastic nomination, Noelle had agreed to substitute. Directing plays she could handle, but appearing in them was a different animal altogether.

Noelle fidgeted with her shoulders, trying to get comfortable despite the gauze wings tied to her back.

"Hold still, dear. I'll fix them. By the way, did I tell you how lovely you look? That silver gown goes well with your pink hair—and the iced glitter you added is a nice touch. Interesting."

Noelle chuckled. Her mother was always determined to unearth the bright side of life. "Have I told you how much I love you, Mom?"

"Not lately," she shot back with a grin.

"Well I do. Love you, I mean."

Her mom's eyes welled up with tears. As if embarrassed, she stepped behind Noelle and began fussing with the wings. "These are still lopsided." Her hands stilled after a moment. "I love you, too, dear."

Noelle smiled upon hearing the soft words and straightened her tinsel halo. Peering through the crack of space between lentil and door, she surveyed the audience. Several residents from the retirement center, there by the children's invitation, filled the front row.

In the second row sat Miranda Fitzgerald, looking pale but recovered. She and the kids had moved into the center yesterday, until Miranda could get back on her feet again. Noelle didn't realize how much she would miss her young guests until they were gone, but she was glad they were back with their mom. Seated next to Miranda was her brother, Jimmy, a gregarious redhead with freckles, and on the other side sat Officer Jack, with one arm looped around Miranda's shoulders. A romance had obviously developed in Hartford Falls.

Noelle sobered when she thought about her own love life.

Since the earth-shaking kiss of four days ago, Todd hadn't tried to kiss her again, though she'd seen him both at church and on Monday, when he delivered a shipment to the craft store. True, neither were opportune times for a kiss, but on both occasions he'd seemed removed, too polite. And yesterday, at dress rehearsal, he'd barely talked to her. Yes, they'd been busy, but this new distance made her wonder. Earlier this evening, she'd caught sight of him standing alone, hands in his back pockets, staring out a window at the faraway mountains and mumbling to himself. Uncertain, she had slipped away, sensing he didn't want company.

From across the room, Cindy motioned to her that it was time to begin, and Noelle turned to the ten-year-old narrator. "Luke, you're on."

The boy nodded, tugged at the bottom ends of his suit coat, and strode onto the stage, head held high. Noelle kept close watch. She winced when Carmen, who played Mary, stumbled on the walk to the manger set, but Jeremy in the role of Joseph grabbed her elbow, saving her. A sight amazing to see, since it seemed those two were always fighting. Noelle listened to the lines, proud of how well the children did. And those without lines didn't miss their cues to act, either.

Noelle straightened. Her own cue was coming up shortly.

"By the way," her mom said, "I almost forgot. Todd asked me to tell you that he needs to speak with you alone after the play. It sounded important. He'll meet you in the rec room."

"What?" Noelle looked back, stunned.

"You're on," came a child's loud whisper.

Noelle blinked, trying to get her bearings. She managed to walk to her spot onstage, where she was to announce to the shepherds the birth of Christ the King. Instead, her mind played back her mother's words.

Focus. Focus.

Somehow, she delivered her lines without a flaw, glided to the back, then hurried to grab the silver glittered star from the backstage table, also hoping for clarification.

Her mother was nowhere in sight.

Noelle sighed and drifted to the backdrop. She took the steps up the short ladder placed there so she could hold the star above the stable. Thankful she'd chosen to be in her stocking feet, to lessen the risk of losing her balance, she propped one hand against the sturdy roof while holding the star high. Todd had done a great job on the set and had pounded in double the amount of nails after their misadventure with the panel that first day.

From her perch, Noelle watched the kids, silently mouthing their lines with them, mentally prodding them when they hesitated. Selena and Scottie made endearing shepherds as they slowly walked and knelt by the manger, Selena holding a stuffed lamb in her arms. As the wise men moved forward with their treasures, Noelle was about to expel a relieved breath when suddenly, three-year-old shepherdess Ginny yawned, laid down her staff, and walked closer to the manger.

Oh, no! Noelle cringed. "No, Ginny, no," she whispered as loudly as she dared.

Her words must have been too soft to reach the child. Ginny, as she'd done before, crawled into the manger with the doll baby Jesus, cuddled it close, and prepared to take a nap.

A few chuckles circulated among the audience. A shocked silence prevailed onstage. Narrator Luke, whose line was to end the play, looked up at Noelle, seeking direction.

Noelle thought fast for a fitting conclusion, in light of what Ginny had done. "And so, every Christmas, people celebrate the love Christ gave to us when He came down to Earth as an innocent babe. And in turn, we share our love with Him."

Someone in the audience began to clap. Others stood, and the clapping grew louder. It was obvious everyone now thought Ginny's act was intentional.

Smiling, Noelle stepped down off the ladder. As far as she was concerned, they would never be the wiser.

Todd stood in the rec room, waiting on Noelle. He hoped she'd gotten the message to join him. He hadn't trusted himself to speak to her earlier. As jumpy as he'd been all day he was sure he would have blown everything if he'd tried. While staring out the window at the faraway pine-clad mountains, he had even rehearsed what he planned to say to her, under his breath.

It began to snow, and he recalled the snow on her hair, her lashes, her shining face. . .

Shifting his attention from the window, he shoved his fingers deep into his pockets. Too bad he couldn't remember the words in the order he'd planned them. Memorization had never been one of his strong points.

The angel-funnel decorations Noelle had helped the children make caught his eye. Later, during the gift exchange, the kids would distribute them to their moms. Brown, beige, and yellow angels dotted the spruce tree's boughs. But none of the angels bore bright pink hair.

Todd grinned when he remembered Selena's comment to Noelle, as they were boxing up the special strawberry-haired angel to send to the kids' former babysitter, whom Todd learned was currently residing in Missouri.

"I know you're not a real angel," Selena had said in all earnestness. "But can I still call you my angel?"

The sweetest, softest expression had lit up Noelle's face, and Todd wished he could have bottled up that look in a jar to remember on the gray days ahead. The next several minutes would determine just how many gray days loomed in his future. Hearing a rustle at the door, he turned and inhaled a slow breath.

Noelle was the most beautiful woman he'd ever seen.

Feeling self-conscious because of his direct stare, Noelle walked toward Todd. She knew she looked ridiculous in the angel getup, but she hadn't wanted to risk taking the time to change and have him get tired of waiting for her then possibly leave.

"The play was a success." His voice sounded strained.

"Yes, thanks to Ginny's finale. I can't believe everyone thought it was planned."

"You saved the play with your ending line. It was great. Happy birthday, by the way."

"Thanks." Why did she suddenly feel so awkward with him?

"Noelle, I've got something I need to say—"

Before he could continue, one of the mothers rushed inside. "Have either of you seen Jeremy? They're cutting the cake, and I don't want him to miss out."

Both Todd and Noelle said no, and Jeremy's mom hurried away. Seconds crawled by.

"You had something you wanted to tell me?" Noelle prompted.

"Yes, I. . ." He pulled his hand from his pocket.

"Hey," Jeremy said as he walked in. "Was my mom just here?"

"Yes," Noelle said. "She's looking for you. They're cutting the cake."

"Great! And, oh yeah. Thanks, Mr. B, for teaching me how to juggle. You're one okay dude." The boy shot out of the room.

"You taught him to juggle?" Noelle gave him a warm smile. Jeremy had no father. Teaching the boy had been a thoughtful gesture on Todd's part, considering the way Jeremy had treated him his first day there.

Todd barely nodded. "Noelle. . ."

"Yes, Todd?"

"There's something I've got to get off my chest. . . ."

Noelle felt confused. He sounded so serious.

"There you two are!" Cindy poked her head in the door. "You're missing all the fun. With the way those kids are wolfing down the goodies, I can't promise there'll be anything left."

"Cindy," Noelle said in a voice that clearly implied she was intruding.

Her friend raised one hand. "Don't mind me. I never said

a word. I wasn't even here." Her words trailed away as she drifted out of sight.

The second she was gone, Todd blurted, "Will you be my angel?"

"Your angel?"

"I mean my girl." He let out a nervous chuckle. "Angel is on the brain for some reason. This is coming out all wrong. And I'd even rehearsed what I planned to say."

Noelle felt as if she were in high school again, only this time the scenario she'd always dreamed of was playing out.

"You want me to be your girl?" she softly asked.

"For now. With the prospect of moving on to something more permanent down the road."

"Permanent?" she squeaked.

"As in marriage. I love you, Noelle."

She was stunned speechless.

"I know it's too early to discuss the future," he hurried to say, "and I doubt I make as much as your former boyfriends, just so you know. But I hope to move up in the company. I plan to take those computer classes Dad suggested, to help me earn a better position—"

"Todd." Without thinking, she laid her fingers against his lips as she said his name. They were warm and soft and she didn't want to move her hand away. But she did, feeling as if she existed in another dimension, one where time had slowed in a beautiful bright-lit, sharp-focused atmosphere. "I don't care about the money. Yes, I want my basic needs met—everyone does—and it would be nice to live comfortably, but I have no desire to marry a Daddy Warbucks."

Todd hiked his brow. "Daddy Warbucks?"

"The millionaire from Annie. I watched the movie with the kids last week." She thought a moment. "Remember when I told you I moved back home because I realized the things I'd been searching for were here all along? We were interrupted and I never answered your question about what those things were."

He nodded.

"I was looking for acceptance and love for the person I am, faults included. And I accept you for the person you are, too." She giggled, awareness fully dawning. "I can't believe we're standing here discussing the possibility of marriage."

"Then it is possible?" Todd said the words as if he couldn't believe them.

"Of course. Don't you know yet that I've loved you ever since I met you? Even more so, now. I just never thought you'd be interested in a pink-haired ditz like me."

He grinned. "The sweetest pink-haired 'ditz' I know."

"Todd." She felt the blush rise to her face.

"I have a birthday present for you." He opened the hand he'd pulled from his pocket. Inside was a gold pendant bearing a reddish-pink carnelian gemstone in the shape of a rose. "I've become fond of the color—and it seemed the perfect keepsake for this Pink Fusion Christmas that brought us together."

"Oh, Todd, it's beautiful." She lifted her hair for him to fasten the necklace around her throat. "I'll always treasure it." Touching the rose, she gazed up into his eyes and saw the love shining there.

He slid his hands around her waist, drawing her close, and kissed her tenderly, leaving Noelle with no doubt that dreams could come true. Especially at Christmastime.

"And I'll always treasure you," he whispered in her ear, "my strawberry angel."

One-of-a-Kind Christmas Angel

Materials listed are a guideline. Other items can be substituted if preferred. This is your unique Christmas angel, so customize to fit your personal taste. All listed items can be found at home, or at your local craft or dollar store. This is a fun craft to make with the kids or grandkids!

Parental supervision is recommended.

You'll need:
- Plastic funnel
- Feathers (or angel wings)
- Styrofoam ball (for head)
- Pipe cleaners
- Twist tie (found on bread wrappers, etc.)
- Tinsel
- Pretty material (for dress)
- Flesh-colored material (for face)
- Glue—both craft glue and hot glue gun
- Fine-point markers
- Ruler
- Tweezers
- Decorations for dress— (i.e., glitter, sequins, ribbon, lace, buttons, etc.)

INSTRUCTIONS:

Body: Cut a circle in pretty material 5 inches bigger than funnel's wide bottom. To measure, place funnel on wrong side of cloth and with ruler, draw equal-sized lines on cloth radiating from funnel. Connect lines at tops, drawing with pencil, to form a circle. Cut slit in center, same width as funnel's narrow top. If material is type to fray, glue with sewing glue, or hem, if desired. Carefully tug slit over top of funnel until secure. This can be used as either a full dress or skirt. If desired, wrap lace or other material around top for bodice. (Picture shows 4 angels to show variety of ideas). Use hot glue at top to anchor, if needed.

Praying hands: Cut a 2-inch by 6-inch piece of same material and fold around flesh-colored pipe cleaner so that 1 inch of pipe cleaner shows at each end. (You may need to cut pipe cleaner.) Glue length of material together all across bottom to form angel's sleeves. Bend to form loop, then bend pipe cleaner ends and twist around each other for praying hands. (In picture, I gave one of my angels a carol book to hold, also made with pipe cleaners). Slip loop over narrow part of funnel at angle, so "shoulders" are at top back and hands rest at waist. Hot glue shoulders to back.

Head: Cut a circle of flesh-colored material big enough to wrap around Styrofoam ball, so that at least 3 inches of material hangs down after it's tied together. Smooth wrinkles from face area and tie off with a twist tie. Draw face with fine-tip markers (i.e., crescents and lashes for closed eyes and O-shaped mouth for singing angel). Crop thickness of excess material if needed—thin it out—but keep length so material can be inserted through funnel top and pulled down from inside. You'll do this by putting your hand inside funnel, so leave enough material hanging to easily grab onto. (You may need to use tweezers.) Pull until head is flush with top of funnel. Use tweezers to gently push down any excess material through hole. Hot glue where head meets funnel, if needed, and glue lace or tinsel around this to form angel's collar if desired.

Hair: Hot glue curly yarn or tassel to top of head. Glue gold or silver tinsel or shiny pipe cleaner around top for halo. (With a tassel, you may want to wrap pipe cleaner around top "hump" if tassel has one and form an elevated halo.)

Decorate as desired. Hot glue feathers to back for wings. Give as a gift, set your one-of-a-kind angel on the mantel, or use as a tree-topper to remind you that God's angels are watching over you this Christmas and always. And have a Merry Christmas!

PAMELA GRIFFIN

Award-winning author Pamela Griffin makes her home in Texas, where snow makes a rare visit at Christmastime, but she doesn't let that fact dampen her holiday cheer. Christmas is her favorite holiday, and she enjoys viewing the lights with her kids, making homemade candy, watching old Christmas movies, and all the rest of the gala that this festive time of year brings—especially the friendly get-togethers and family reunions. She loves to write and has written several stories set during the Christmas season. Multi-published, with close to thirty novels and novellas, she gives God the glory for every amazing thing He's done in her writing career. She invites you to drop by and visit her Web site at: http://users.waymark.net/words_of_honey.

Angel
Charm

by Tamela Hancock Murray

Charm is deceptive, and beauty is fleeting;
but a woman who fears the Lord is to be praised.

PROVERBS 31:30 NIV

Chapter 1

Standing on the back porch of Charming Manor, Lydia Winters mulled over the celebrations scheduled for the year: Back-to-School Night, Thanksgiving, Christmas, Valentine's Day. . .

Valentine's Day. She couldn't remember the last time she'd celebrated the occasion with a date.

"Funny. Charm is my stock-in-trade and yet I wasn't charming enough to keep the love of my life." Lydia ran her fingertip over the rim of her half-empty glass of sweetened iced tea. Perhaps the hint of coolness in the Missouri air, with its promise of a new school year on the horizon, reminded her of the past that had set her mind afire.

She shook memories of Drake Kingston out of her head. Whatever prompted such a thought had to go. Present concerns left no time for such romanticizing about a distant time and place. Drake had long since left the Midwest and hadn't been a part of her life for over fifteen years. He was gone for good. She'd heard talk about his recent plans to return to help his mother recover from recent hip replacement surgery. He had married a woman from his adopted state of New York years ago. Surely he and his wife were happy. She hoped so.

She finished the rest of her tea and mulled over the roster of new students for fall. Running over the final count in her head, she realized all of her classes at Charming Manor were full. Space for a few newcomers would have to be created, a situation that presented itself every year and tested her ability to remain charming under pressure. Finding more slots never proved easy since Lydia's school was located in the house she had inherited from her maternal grandparents. Perhaps the aged four-bedroom frame home, which she had painted pale pink with fuchsia shutters, wasn't really a manor. But to Lydia, living alone in such quarters made her house feel larger than it was. Certainly the two acres surrounding the place, with its vegetable and rose gardens thriving next to the lush green yard she tended, provided more than enough outdoor work to fill her mornings.

"Lydia!"

Hearing an unexpected male voice, Lydia gave a start as

she spotted a stocky man wearing a light blue short-sleeved shirt, a dark blue cap, and matching shorts, the uniform of the U.S. Postal Service. She exhaled. "Oh, it's you, Ralph."

He ascended three of the five wooden porch steps painted fuchsia to meet her more than halfway. "Sorry to surprise you, Miss Lydia."

"That's quite all right." Lydia smiled, partly at the way he called her "Miss Lydia" even though he had lived a year or two past the half-century mark. In fact, most of the people she knew called her Miss Lydia, despite the fact everyone knew she hadn't seen her thirty-fifth birthday. She sensed they enjoyed the idea of a resident expert on etiquette, and the amiable honorific seemed to fit.

"You sure must have had your mind on something, to let me sneak up on you like that."

"You're right. I was preoccupied, Ralph."

"No doubt about tonight's party. I'm sure everyone there will have loads of fun. Seems like you'll be having a full house. I saw right many RSVPs come back to you."

"They did." Not wishing to comment on the degree of knowledge he was willing to share about her mail, she kept her voice terse and answer brief.

He smiled and held out a package. "I wanted to make sure you got this."

"A package? Wonder what it is. I haven't ordered anything

lately." Lydia set her empty tumbler down on the glass top of a green wrought iron table and remembered her manners. "May I offer you a glass of tea?"

"Thanks for the invitation." Ralph took off his hat and wiped his sweaty brow with it. "Sure is tempting, but I don't have time to stop today." After placing his hat back over a bald spot peeking through strands of hair that appeared to have benefited from liberal application of black dye, Ralph extended the other hand to relinquish the box.

Lydia looked for the return address.

"No return address," Ralph offered, as if reading her mind. "Wonder who it's from."

She turned the package over, searching for a clue. "I have no idea."

"You don't say?" He folded his arms. "Who'd go to all the trouble and expense to mail a package and then not say on the front who it's from? What if your address was wrong? Or what if you'd moved too long ago for the U.S. Postal Service to forward the package? Without a return address, we couldn't send it back. Then whoever it is would think you got the package and then wonder why they never got an answer. They'd have nothing to show for their efforts but a package they didn't know ended up in the Dead Letter Post Office, and no way to reach you on top of that."

"You have a point."

Obviously encouraged by her acquiescence, Ralph puffed out his chest and emboldened the volume of his voice. "If I had my druthers, I wouldn't even deliver a piece of mail without a return address. To my way of thinking, there's no reason not to put a return address. Unless you've got something to hide."

"I certainly don't have anything to hide," Lydia assured him. "And I always use a return address label."

His voice softened. "I know that much, Miss Lydia. Your labels are mighty pretty, too, what with those pink roses you've got on 'em. The perfect flower for a pretty lady like yourself." Lydia surmised that most men who hadn't been given a lick of encouragement would have flushed a bit, or at least averted their eyes for an instant after delivering such a bold pass, but not Ralph.

"Thank you, Ralph." Since he kept looking into her face, she felt obligated to return the favor with a lukewarm sentiment. "What a nice thing to say." Employing discouraging body language to keep him from ascending the remaining two steps, she clutched the box to her chest.

"It's the truth, I tell you." He grinned as he reached into the blue satchel hanging from his shoulder and extracted the rest of her mail. Lydia noticed several catalogs and a few envelopes. Rather than handing them to her, he tapped the rolled up mail on the side of his leg. "So you've got no idea who sent that box, huh?"

"Really, I don't." Her grip on the parcel tightened.

"Well, you're too popular to have any enemies. Although I did notice the postmark is from Independence. You didn't have an argument with somebody there, did you? I sure hope not. A big town like that—especially so close to Kansas City and everything—can harbor an awful lot of nuts."

A half chuckle escaped her lips. "Thank you for your concern, but no, I haven't argued with anyone in Independence."

"I hope not." He tilted his head eastward. "They're close enough for someone to get at you if they set their mind to it."

She chose to ignore the sinister half of his remark and kept her voice cheerful. "Yes, I do recall my state geography."

"I know. I know. Just a reminder, that's all." He sighed. "I guess it's not something that will hurt you. I held your package up to my ear just to be sure, and I didn't hear any ticking sound."

Lydia was amused in spite of herself. She tried not to smile. "Thank you, Ralph."

"Sure is mysterious." He scratched his forehead under the rim of his cap.

"Surely it is." Lydia grinned. He was still tapping the rest of her mail on the side of his leg. If he continued, she speculated he might wear a hole in the top of his blue knee sock. "You're not going to give me the rest of my mail until I open this, are you?"

He shook his head. "Uh-uh."

"All right, then. Come on up."

As expected he leapt onto the porch. Lydia bit her lip to keep from suggesting to Ralph that he might benefit from a semester at Charming Manor as she seated herself on a wrought iron chair that matched the table. She set the package in her lap and studied it. Brown wrapping offered no clues. A plain white label bore her address in bold typeface. The box was compact and lightweight enough to be empty. But who would mail an empty box?

Lydia realized that sliding her fingernail under the packing tape was certain to mar the modest French manicure she had applied earlier that morning. She wanted her nails to appear well groomed but not too daring for the party. She would need her silver letter opener. "I'll be right back, Ralph." She rose from her seat. "Are you sure you won't take a glass of tea? I'll be passing through the kitchen to retrieve my letter opener."

He shook his head. "Nope. Don't have time."

Lydia turned before he could see her grin. If he spent this much time at all of his stops, no wonder Ralph ran late almost every day. Once indoors, she glided through the recently renovated kitchen filled with the aromas of cookies, cherry pies, and puff pastries, and noted that the last plate of chocolate chip oatmeal cookies she had baked appeared to be cooling nicely. A short trip through the hall took her into the study in the back part of the house.

Since her mahogany desk gleamed, free of clutter, Lydia immediately located her letter opener in the top left drawer. Spying one of her long, ash-blond strands of hair hanging from one of the rhinestones set in the handle, Lydia grimaced as she removed the offender and let it float into an empty carved mahogany wastebasket. She slid the silver blade underneath a beige swath of unyielding packing tape. When it wouldn't give way, she stabbed the tape with the tip of the opener. The gap allowed the blade to slice through tough plastic.

"Whoever sent this wanted to make me work to get inside," she mused.

She tore off the brown outer wrapping. Underneath was another layer of paper, this time a green foil.

"That's quite a color contrast," she muttered. "Looks like Christmas in August."

Curiosity aroused, she would have kept going except that she had an audience waiting outside. Nosy or not, Ralph was being a friend to look after her and her mysterious package. For that reason she owed him the consideration of letting him see its contents.

"Careful, Scarlett," she told the white Persian who had snuck into the study. The last time Lydia had accidentally caught Scarlett's tail in the door, the poor cat had avoided her for a week. Once in the hall, Lydia heard her other cat, a Siamese, mewing. "Rhett's waiting for you." The two cats disappeared up the stairs.

When she returned to the porch she discovered Ralph still waiting, leaning against a fuchsia column. His gaze rested on the package. "So what's somebody doing sending you a Christmas gift this early?"

"That's what I'm hoping we're about to find out." Lydia took her place back in the chair. Sliding the letter opener underneath a flap of foil wrap, Lydia removed the green paper and discovered a white box.

"Still seems suspicious to me," Ralph commented. "Where's the name of the store?"

She looked and discovered the moniker CHRISTMAS FOREVER and on the next line, KANSAS CITY, KANSAS on the lower corner, scripted in red. "Must be a store that sells Christmas items all year round." She lifted the lid and took the object, wrapped in tissue, out of the box.

After unwinding what seemed to be an entire batch of tissue, she discovered a round Christmas ornament. On it was stamped a picture of an old-fashioned house, a two-story frame structure much like Charming Manor, amid snow falling in twilight. A horse drawn carriage awaited its occupants. Lydia imagined a party taking place, with everyone sipping hot cocoa topped with sweet whipped cream and munching salted popcorn. The scene sent happy chills through her as she remembered winters past. For a moment, the heat of Indian summer, with its outdoor smells of mowed lawns and gathered hay, dissipated into recollections of the comforting aroma of roasting turkey and the crisp odor of a balsam pine Christmas tree.

She sighed. "It's beautiful!"

Ralph adjusted his silver-rimmed sunglasses and peered at the bulb. "Yep. Sure is."

A note had been placed underneath the ornament. She read it to herself: FROM YOUR SECRET ADMIRER.

"What's it say?" Ralph prodded.

Lydia wasn't sure how to answer. She felt the flush of heat around her collar. "It's rather silly, really. A joke, more than likely."

"A joke?" He set his fist on his thigh. "I don't like the sound of that."

Lydia decided that working Ralph up into a dither over nothing wasn't worth keeping a harmless confidence. "All right. I'll tell you. It says it's from a secret admirer." She let out a practiced giggle to show her embarrassment. "Isn't that the silliest thing you ever heard?"

"I don't see anything silly about it. Nothing silly at all."

As Ralph studied her, Lydia became conscious of her old blue jeans and white oxford blouse fashioned of cotton that had seen one washing too many. Clothes good enough for baking, but not for company. Not even the postman.

"So," Ralph said, "are you gonna put it somewhere on your tree?"

She shrugged. "I suppose so. I don't see why not."

"Depends on whether or not you find out who the secret admirer is, and if you like him well enough, huh?"

"Whoever the admirer is, he has excellent taste. I think I'll put it on the tree regardless."

"Well, that's mighty nice of you. Charming, in fact." He grinned at his own wit. "I guess it wouldn't do me much harm to get a few new ornaments myself. I have a plastic star on the top of my tree every year. It started out red, but you can see silver now where the paint's peeled off in a couple of places. But nobody notices the difference once you get it on the tree. They're all too busy looking for the loot underneath, anyway."

"Now, Ralph. You know there's much more to Christmas than that."

"Maybe to you, but you'll have a hard time convincing most postal carriers—that's the politically correct term. They don't let us call ourselves mailmen anymore. Anyway, my buddies know that gifts are a big part of Christmas whether anyone but the retailers wants to admit it or not. Our bags are so heavy with catalogs before Christmas and we're so loaded down with boxes at Christmas, that we know gift giving is a big part of all the fuss. Too big a part, in my book."

"It can be for some people," Lydia conceded. "I admit, I get caught up in all the consumerism too much sometimes myself. When I do, I try to make a point of spending more time in devotional reading to refocus myself on what's important."

"That's a fine idea, Miss Lydia. No wonder everyone around here thinks you're a fine lady."

"Thank you." Good. Ralph must not have thought she sounded self-righteous when she spoke about her time with the Lord.

He suddenly seemed to remember the rest of her mail. "Well, all this stuff you got today won't help you keep from shopping. You got a whole batch of mail order catalogs. Some even have Santa Claus on the cover." He shook his head as he handed her the mail. "Oh, and you got a postcard from your Aunt Beverly in Florida. Says she had a wonderful time with her Bible group in Jerusalem. Didn't get sick once from the food. Good for her." He gave Lydia a toothy smile.

She took the mail from him. "Thank you." Anywhere else, Ralph would probably have been turned in to his supervisor for reading the mail. She decided not to make a point of that fact. After all, her friendly postman meant well.

Chapter 2

L ovely party, Miss Lydia."

"Thank you, Ashlynn." The redhead had been one of Lydia's favorite pupils the previous year. She set her gaze for a moment on a similar version of Ashlynn standing just out of earshot. "I look forward to having your sister in my class."

"And she can't wait to begin classes with you as well." Ashlynn sent her the type of self-assured and pleasant smile that Lydia had taught her well.

Mission accomplished.

As Lydia checked the banquet table to make sure plenty of sweetened tea filled the pitchers, she overheard the voice of one of her new students, Jennifer. "I don't know why you wouldn't want to take lessons here, Kelly. Everybody who's anybody around here goes to Miss Lydia's school."

Kelly? Lydia wondered silently. So that was the name of the girl with the harsh makeup and vivid hair, the girl who would have stuck out in any crowd, but most certainly within this group of young ladies she planned to teach the niceties of life. No one with that name had appeared on Lydia's invitation roster. She had assumed the new girl was a friend of one of her present students. She'd been waiting for someone to remember her manners and to introduce them. Yet none of the girls claimed to be Kelly's friend.

Then who was she?

Brushing a few stray crumbs from the white damask tablecloth into her open palm, Lydia refrained from shooting Jennifer a chastening look. As much as Lydia appreciated the compliment about her school, Jennifer would have to be taught not to appear as a snob.

Nearing the cut crystal punch bowl, Lydia cut her gaze to the two teens. Jennifer was eating from a plate overloaded with slices of pecan pie, cherry cheesecake, and cookies. Lydia made another mental note about Jennifer. She would have to be taught the niceties of delicate eating, at least in public.

Beside Jennifer was the girl Lydia now knew as Kelly. Lydia cut furtive glances her way to keep her study of the girl from becoming obvious. Kelly held no plate, but kept her arms folded across her chest, barely concealing what appeared to be the logo of a music group. Judging from several skulls and drops of blood, she assumed the group played hard rock. A cloud as dark as Kelly's hair seemed to be upon the girl.

"Then I guess I don't care if I'm anybody or not," Lydia heard Kelly say.

Unable to bear the girl's distress, Lydia interrupted. "Good evening, Jennifer."

The blond's face brightened. "Good evening, Miss Lydia. I was just telling Kelly how wonderful it is to go to your school. I'm looking so forward to your classes."

Jennifer had all the right words down but her tone sounded too icky sweet to convey sincerity. Lydia would have to coach her on not appearing shallow. She decided the lesson could wait.

"I'm glad to hear that, Jennifer." Lydia turned to Kelly. "I don't believe we've met."

Instead of answering, Kelly pushed her hair behind her ear, revealing four ear piercings decorated with alternating studs and small silver hoops.

"Oh, excuse me," Jennifer said. "Kelly Kingston, allow me to introduce you to our headmistress, Miss Lydia Winters."

Kingston?

Kingston? Lydia swallowed and composed her mouth

into a line that wouldn't betray her shock. Her beating heart reminded her of old feelings she thought she had long ago buried. Then again, an image of Drake had popped into her mind just that morning. *No, it can't be the same Kingston family. This is obviously a coincidence.*

"Miss Lydia?" Jennifer asked. "Is everything all right?"

Lydia forced herself to smile. "Certainly, Jennifer."

Those eyes, black as night. They look so much like Drake's. No, it must be my imagination.

Jennifer beamed. "Kelly says she'll be a student here this semester."

"That's if my dad can get me in." Kelly refused to accept Lydia's extended hand or to smile. "But if there aren't any more slots, I'll understand."

Before Lydia could comment, an unmistakable male voice she hadn't heard in years interrupted. "Lydia's an old friend of mine. She'll make room for you, Kelly."

Lydia turned and found herself gazing into ebony eyes she remembered from long ago. Drake's masculine face remained unlined. The straight, pointed nose, mouth that looked as though it was ready to grin at any moment, impish black curls—were all as she remembered. The years seemed to dissolve, along with everyone else in the room. All Lydia could see was Drake. The man who had broken her heart.

Drake tried not to stare. He hadn't approached Lydia until that moment, instead choosing to remain on the porch. As he caught up with other old friends, he had further justified his reticence by rationalizing that she needed to mingle with new students. But in reality, he had been too nervous to go inside. Now close to her, he saw that Lydia appeared even more beautiful than he remembered. His mind took him back fifteen years, to another era.

In high school, she had been a tiny little thing, wispy and shy. But during the summer between their junior and senior years, her parents had sent her to some sort of charm school in Kansas City. He remembered the first day of school during senior year. He hadn't known why at the time, but she had blossomed into a different person. Change was evident on the outside. Her clothes had always been fine as far as he was concerned. He liked how she appeared casual in a T-shirt, usually white, and blue jeans. Her new clothes were still informal but appeared much crisper and made her look more like a young woman on a mission than a teenager worried about homework or getting to her next class. He liked how polished she appeared. Her image hadn't been just a picture on the outside. When he talked to her, he had noticed she didn't shuffle her feet or avoid his gaze.

Quickly he fell in love with the new presentation. And just as quickly, she had broken his heart.

He looked back at her now. As poised and polished as ever, she looked even more natural and possessed of fewer airs than she had in high school. Her cheeks, lips, and eyes looked natural, not artificial. A sleeveless dress in a soft blue hugged her curves.

Emotions that evoked an anticipatory shiver and a pleasant roll of his stomach reminded him of the feelings he experienced that September day so long ago. Lydia Winters looked as ravishing as ever.

Winters. Her maiden name. His mom said she never married, even hinted he was the reason why. He prayed that wasn't so.

"It's good to see you again, Lydia." He hoped he had hit the right combination of friendliness yet aloofness.

"You too, Drake."

Her smile seemed so practiced that he couldn't imagine such a cultured woman pining away over anyone all these years. Least of all, him. Mom had to be dead wrong. Too bad.

He poured water on the fiery emotion as soon as it left his subconscious. What was he thinking? He swallowed and tried to compose his expression into one that said he was interested in her only as his daughter's potential charm school teacher. He nodded toward the girls. "So you have a full roster this year?"

"Yes, I am pleased to say."

He allowed his gaze to observe the dining room. "Maybe you should move to larger quarters."

She stiffened. "I'm fine here, thank you. I like to keep my classes small. And I enjoy my place here at Charming Manor."

"We do, too, Miss Lydia," one of the girls, a blond, piped up.

Drake held back a grimace. Great. Not two sentences had left his mouth before he was dispensing advice he had no right to give. No wonder Lydia's chin tilted at him in the defiant way he remembered it used to do whenever she felt miffed. He tried to recover. "I can see why. Come to think of it, your grandmother lived in this house, didn't she?"

"Yes. I inherited this place from her. I suppose it's hardly recognizable since I painted it pink."

"I really like it pink," the blond remarked.

"Thank you, Jennifer," Lydia said.

"I'll have to say, the color does add its own brand of unique appeal." He eyed a mahogany table. "I'm glad to see you still have most of her furniture. Antiques are the only type of pieces that would suit this place."

"I daresay contemporary furniture would seem strange here."

"I agree." A contented sigh escaped him. "I remember that Christmas Eve party she had here. Your grandmother made the best hot cocoa. And do you remember how the whole world seemed covered with snow that night?" The images in his mind took him back so much he looked over to the fireplace, expecting a fire. He almost felt surprised to see no logs burning.

"Yes, I do seem to remember something about that." Her voice didn't convey the tone of a woman reminiscing. Terseness stiffened her face. "A perfect scene. Someone almost could have painted a picture of it."

"Yeah. Someone like Norman Rockwell. Or Thomas Kinkade." He smiled, but instead of returning his smile she cocked her head and studied him.

She turned her attention to her students. "I meant to ask if you girls have tried the jelly roll. Would you like to learn how to make that during one of our cooking classes?"

"I'd love to try it!" the blond replied, not surprising Drake.

Another non-surprise was the way Kelly's dark eyes rolled toward the ceiling and back. His rebellious daughter looked the part, but none of her teachers ever accused her of being stupid. She could spot a fake with no trouble.

"I'll bet the jelly roll is delicious, Kelly. Try some."

She twisted her bright red lips and narrowed her eyes

at him to show she knew exactly what he was doing—getting rid of her—but acquiesced. That talk about being on her best behavior was paying dividends. She had agreed in exchange for being allowed to wear those horrible clothes.

Drake let out a deliberate chuckle. "Yes. I seem to remember it was white with black shutters. Not very imaginative." He felt himself blanch. In trying to compliment Lydia, he had insulted her grandmother's taste. At least the girls hadn't heard his gaffe. "Nothing against your granny."

She laughed. "Granny was a practical old bird. She'd be horrified by what I've done here. But I think it's perfect for a charm school."

"So do I." He'd trudged so far into the verbal mud that he figured he might as well see if quicksand awaited. "So your significant other doesn't mind a pink house?"

"Significant other? The only significant other in my life is the Lord, Drake."

Oh, good! He cleared his throat. "There's no one on the horizon?"

"No." For the first time that evening, she took a sudden interest in her white, heeled sandals. "But I'm perfectly happy. Perfectly happy." Her crisp voice suggested otherwise.

What could he say? "Um, I'm glad to hear that."

This was not going well. He felt like such an idiot. He should have been more pressing when he asked his mother to catch him up on news in the town before he went to the party. But he hadn't wanted to seem too eager to see Lydia. Not even in front of his mother. She'd always loved Lydia, which had most likely been a prompt for her to mention Lydia's school to him. He'd managed to play it cool so far, but his mother would be sure to pounce on any hint of his interest beyond Kelly's welfare.

His happiness about her freedom evaporated in light of the way her chin tilted again and her emerald eyes looked as hard as those precious stones. He almost wished he hadn't broached the subject. There weren't too many ways out and none of them looked good. He decided to try the road that promised an exit. "I know my daughter Kelly will enjoy her lessons."

"Kelly." She looked over at the girls.

Drake's gaze followed hers. Kelly stood out in any crowd, but she appeared to be more of an outcast in her current environment than usual. Several teenagers milled near her, and like the shallow blond, they all looked as though they had already seen a few semesters of charm school. Their outfits matched, their hair was styled to make them seem as though they belonged in a fashion magazine, and they wore pleasant expressions.

Kelly leaned against a wall. Surely slumping violated etiquette. Still, he felt thankful. He knew Kelly well enough to realize she had summoned all her will to keep her mouth from curving downward and her glance from rolling to the ceiling.

"Yes, Kelly is all mine." He flashed her his best smile and made sure his voice displayed the right amount of fatherly pride. "I'm sure she'll benefit greatly from your school."

Doubt flooded Lydia's green eyes.

Drake wished he could do or say something to remove all of her anxiety, but Kelly's obvious lack of recognizable charm left him with little leeway.

Returning his glance to Lydia, he sensed she didn't need a knight in shining armor despite her barely contained regret that no prince hitched a white horse to a post in the driveway. He wondered why. Standing before him was a slim but fuller figured woman than the teenager he remembered. Years had done nothing to etch around her eyes with wrinkles or harden her face. Nor did she seem dragged down from the cares of life. Who wouldn't want to marry such a beautiful, charming, and successful woman? Such a contrast to his daughter. Could Lydia make Kelly more like her?

"Uh, I know she's a bit edgy looking. But she has a wonderful heart. Really," he assured Lydia.

"I'm sure she does." Her tone didn't indicate much confidence. "I'm afraid I have a full enrollment. I'll have to squeeze her in if I am able to take her at all. And I have a couple of other girls on the waiting list ahead of her."

His stomach seemed to pound the bottom of his gut. After all these years, couldn't she make special accommodations for him? Then again, maybe not. Maybe he didn't have the right even to think such a thing. "Oh, please." He didn't like the whining tone of his own voice, but he couldn't suppress it. "Don't let our past—"

"I'm a professional. I would never let any past relationship I had with a young woman's parent be a consideration, either for or against school admission." She bristled.

"I know that. I didn't mean to offend you." He pressed his thumbs against the outside of his pants pockets. "It's just that, it's so hard without her mother."

He looked at Lydia's unlined face. Perhaps she seemed so carefree because she had never married—or given birth to a beautiful baby who turned into a rebellious teenager. Yet Drake sensed her rebellion hadn't reached the core of her soul. He prayed it never would.

He wished he could take Lydia out for a cup of coffee so they could talk. But he couldn't. He couldn't burden her with his problems. Better to let Lydia get to know Kelly for herself without him expressing his own doubts about her—and himself. He suppressed a sardonic smile. Perhaps he, not Lydia, was the one in need of rescue.

"Oh. I didn't realize you're a single parent." Her mouth

slackened and her eyes took on a stricken light but she seemed to recover without delay. "That's okay. I may be teaching an old-fashioned art, but I know a lot of people are divorced nowadays."

"Not divorced. Widowed."

"Oh." The stricken look returned. "I'm sorry."

"That's okay. She's been gone nearly twelve years now."

"No it isn't. It's never okay." Her hand twitched as though she wanted to reach out to him, but she clenched her fingers together instead.

"Thank you for understanding." He deliberately pasted a smile on his face. "I can see why your school is such a success. You obviously know what to say to make a person feel better. So will you find it in your heart to take Kelly on as one of your students?"

"You are aware that this course doesn't last a week or two."

"Yes. It goes all year, after school and some Saturdays."

"Correct. I recommend that my students stay with me throughout the school year. Will you be here that long?"

He nodded. "Yes. Maybe we'll be here forever."

"Forever. That's a very long time."

Forever. That sounded good to his ears. Did Lydia feel the same?

"All right, then. I'll let you know as soon as I can," Lydia promised.

"Good. She needs you." Having blurted more than he meant, Drake made a point of taking a sudden interest in a batch of cookies. If he told Lydia the truth, maybe she wouldn't take Kelly. His daughter had been unhappy at the prospect of leaving her friends in upstate New York—friends he didn't like. No matter that Mom didn't really need him so much. He had come to a point in his life where he needed her—to help him with his daughter.

Not that the apple had fallen far from the tree. Maybe Lydia would give him another chance. He had changed. If she would let him show her how much, she wouldn't be disappointed.

Chapter 3

As the evening drew to a close, Lydia milled around the dining room. Determined to keep her promise to Drake to give him an answer about Kelly, she kept a close eye on the younger girl. Lydia accepted young men but none had shown interest in her school this semester. The girls who had applied possessed evident potential and promised to be eager students.

Kelly was different. If the word "anti-charm" were to appear in the dictionary, Kelly's picture would illustrate the term to perfection. Lydia could see by the way she had applied purple and black makeup and attention-grabbing clothes that she was trying hard to express her rebellion. The girl cried for help. Couldn't anyone else see?

In spite of herself, Kelly's beauty shone through her

tough attitude punctuated by ears with multiple piercings. Always willing to look beyond the surface, Lydia hoped Kelly's reticence would prove temporary and she would become bubbly as the evening progressed. Yet even as the hours passed, Lydia could see that Kelly appeared at Charming Manor against her will and failed to make new friends with ease. She halfway paid attention to others who tried to talk to her, and even from across the room Lydia could tell that Kelly answered their queries in monosyllables. Lips painted bright reddish purple made their tightness all too evident. On the opposite side of the room—and on the opposite side of the spectrum— Drake laughed with one of the parents who had gone to school with them both.

Lord, what should I do? Should I help Drake with Kelly? Or will I do more harm than good?

The Lord didn't wait to give her a sense of what she should do. She needed to help Kelly. He wasn't going to let Lydia escape her responsibilities.

Lord, help me fight any romantic emotions I feel. Drake is no good for me. He wasn't then. He isn't now. I just know it. Help!

Temporary help arrived in the form of a parent with a question. Lydia put off thinking about Kelly and the problems the girl—and her father—promised to present.

The following morning, Lydia drained the last bit of her coffee when she heard a knock. She walked to the door and peeped through the window covered by sheers. "Drake!" She peered at her reflection in the foyer mirror. Her crisp white blouse, black pants, and flat shoes looked satisfactory, but she wished she had splashed a little color on her cheeks and lips before making coffee so company wouldn't catch her with a bare face. Drake knocked once more. She didn't have time for a last-minute makeup fix. He would have to take her as she was.

When she opened the door, her traitorous heart beat hard as she became drenched in the dark pools of his eyes.

Clad in jeans and a fresh denim shirt, he leaned against the side of the door frame with the easy confidence she remembered. "I hope you don't mind my dropping by like this. I couldn't wait. I have to know what you think. Are we students here or not?"

"There's nothing like getting to the point, is there?" She debated whether to invite him in and decided she'd better not.

"No use beating around the bush."

Lydia stalled. "I'm not sure Kelly needs charm school, if she's anything like you. Last night you barely had a spare minute, so many people wanted to see you."

"They're curious as to why I came back after all these years."

"I doubt they're curious. I have a feeling they already know."

"Because of my mom." He looked at the tip of his boot.

Sensing this conversation might take a few moments, Lydia motioned toward two white wicker chairs. Drake didn't hesitate to seat himself.

"Yes. Everybody has been talking about how she's been hobbling around after that hip replacement surgery. But she's been getting along much better than I ever could have thought possible. I can't believe how quickly she's recovering." Lydia paused. "Care for a cup of coffee?"

He waved once. "No. I had some already, thanks."

Lydia took her own seat.

Drake nodded. "I was happy with how well the surgery went."

"Everyone's been helping. Except I haven't had a chance to do much myself. She's so popular and all. I have been keeping up with her progress through the neighbors, though."

As soon as she spoke the words, she realized how defensive she sounded. If she could have looked charming while smacking herself on the forehead, she would have at that moment. Drake had already referred to their past, and that should have served to clear the slate. So why had she made a veiled reference to things best left forgotten? His mother had been sorry to see them break up, and everyone knew it. Lydia felt too awkward to maintain any contact with Mrs. Kingston. Lydia darted her glance toward a massive oak tree in the yard, hoping against hope to find someone in dire need of emergency etiquette lessons so she could rush over and administer first aid in an ever so charming manner.

Ha! Look in the mirror. You haven't done such a great job of being an example, have you?

Drake cut into her self-chastisement. "I did come back to help my mother, and I've appreciated everyone's concern about her health. They're genuine. I can tell."

"I know they are. Everybody around here knows your business, but they care about you. Not like New York, I'd venture."

He thought for a moment. "It was sort of like that in my part of New York. Sure, I didn't know everybody in the Albany-Schenectady-Troy area, but I made friends easily with my immediate neighbors and we all looked out for each other. Upstate is nothing like Manhattan."

"So I've heard."

He cut his glance to her. "You don't have to tell me what you're thinking. You're thinking that Kelly seems like she comes from Manhattan—or, judging from all that makeup, maybe Mars."

"Manhattan. Mars. It's all the same." She chuckled.

"And they'd say, 'Missouri. Mars. It's all the same.'"

Lydia didn't hold back her mirth. "No doubt."

"Sometimes I wonder if they aren't all the same, seriously," Drake confessed. "I tried to shelter Kelly, but it didn't work. She still rebelled and turned from the little girl I knew into an alien."

"That's called being a teenager. At least she agreed to go to the party last night."

"I think it was more to get away from Mother than because she wanted to be here. Oh, I guess I shouldn't have said that." Drake let out a small groan.

"That's okay. I'm not testing you on how charming you are." She winked, and her reward was a smile. "Besides, I need to know the truth about her attitude in regard to taking lessons with me. My course is detailed, and I want my students to enjoy it."

"She will."

"Even if it kills her, huh?"

"I know it's obvious she's a handful. Frankly, that fact embarrasses me. I didn't want her to turn out that way." His gaze bored into her eyes. "And I'm not like that. Not anymore."

"I—I hadn't made the comparison." She tightened her grip on the armrests.

"How kind of you to pretend to forget." His voice was soft. "I want you to know that since I knew you all those years ago, I found Christ."

A happy little gasp escaped her lips. "You did?"

"Yes." If one of the great masters of art had painted Drake's picture to capture that moment in time, Lydia imagined that a light of the palest shade of yellow would emanate from around his face. She had seen that look of rapture in other Christians. His conversion surely had been sincere.

So the cross hanging on a chain that fell just above the open collar of his shirt was more than a fashion statement.

Her heart shattered.

Why couldn't you have found Him when I loved you back then?

"Well," he prodded, "aren't you happy for me?"

She set her mouth into her most attractive smile. "Of course I am. Welcome to the Christian community, my brother in Christ."

"Thanks, but I'm not quite that new at it. I made the altar call years ago. Before Mandy. . ." He looked at the beige rug.

"Your wife." She felt a catch in her throat.

"Yes. That's what's really wrong with Kelly, I think. She

never knew her mother. Maybe I should have moved back here then, and at least Mother could have raised her. But I was too busy working, trying to provide her with a good school and home. And what did I get?"

"A goth."

A shadow of a bittersweet smile passed over his lips. "I didn't think you'd know the term."

"Do I seem as out of it as all that?"

"No. You just seem too sweet to deal with the dark side of teens."

"Judging from the looks of her makeup, I take it you mean that literally."

He laughed. The sound lightened her mood as much as she suspected it cheered him. "I suppose that's right." All too soon he turned serious. "I thought by taking her to church every Sunday, I'd be protecting her. But somehow she still managed to connect with a bad crowd. I desperately wanted to do something, but what? I couldn't just quit my job and babysit her twenty-four seven."

"Of course not." She didn't resist the urge to lean over and set a comforting hand on his shoulder. "You did the best you could. And you still are. Look at how you picked up everything and moved here, just for her sake."

"If I can convince her to stay here."

"Don't be silly. You're her parent. She stays here if you

say so, right? Unless she has other relatives to go to in New York."

"No. I guess that's some comfort, believe it or not. Once Mandy died, her side of the family didn't want much to do with us, especially once Kelly started rebelling."

Lydia looked for something comforting to say, and found it. "It could be worse. They could be taking you to court to gain custody."

"True. There's no danger in that, at least. Mandy's parents are more than happy living as empty nesters. They enjoy the freedom. And her sisters are bogged down with broods of their own. They're too polite to say so, but I'm sure they welcome the limited contact with Kelly for their kids since they think she'd be a negative influence."

"That's too bad. I see the light in her eyes. I don't think she's hard core."

"That's some consolation," he admitted. "Now if only I can get her away from that crowd in New York. She's pining away for all of her friends. I can't keep her off the phone, and when she's not talking on that, she's chatting with them over the Internet. I've already grounded her for the rest of the week from the phone as it is."

"I wouldn't. That could be a huge mistake."

"Really?"

"Yes. Don't try to stop her. That will only make it worse.

For a teen like Kelly, forbidden friendships will just seem more appealing. Maybe she can make friends at church. I—I know your mother doesn't go to church much."

He shook his head.

"Then she won't mind if I invite you to go with me. I attend His Holiness on Main Street. Our pastor offers a contemporary service at ten and a traditional service later. Maybe Kelly would find the contemporary service appealing—or at least less off-putting—since they play modern praise hymns then. You wouldn't believe how many kids go to that service. Some she's already met here last night. The youth group is very active."

"You should go out and pitch your church door to door. You'd fill up the seats so fast they'd have to add an evening service, too."

"Thanks, but we already have one." She took a sudden interest in the small pearl ring she wore on her right ring finger. "I, uh, I didn't mean to come on so strong."

"You didn't," he assured her. "Or at least, I don't mind. I do have one question, though."

She looked up. "What?"

"Does the youth group have any other goths?"

The query sent Lydia into giggles. "Well, they don't dress like that at church, but I'm sure she'll find something in common with someone."

He nodded. "Maybe she will."

"I'll call the head of the church group tomorrow and find out what they have on their agenda. Maybe they'll be going to an amusement park or somewhere she'd like to go. Even if she doesn't make friends right away, she'll still be doing something fun that will get her mind off New York."

"That's a great idea. Thanks for the suggestion. I really appreciate your help. Even though this is my hometown, it's still not so easy getting acclimated to life here again. I've been gone a long time."

Too long. She shook the treacherous thought out of her mind.

"So which service do you go to?" he asked.

She paused. Should she admit that she attended the early service, and that she swayed and clapped her hands to the praise music with as much enthusiasm as the kids half her age? Surely that idea wouldn't hold with her image as a staid etiquette expert. But then again, he hadn't known her as an etiquette expert. He had only known her as a carefree, love-besotted teenager. "I go to the contemporary service."

"Good. Then we'll know someone there." An unsure look entered his expression. "If you don't mind us barging into your Sunday service."

"It's hardly *my* Sunday service. And even if it were, I wouldn't stop you and Kelly from taking part. I don't invite just anyone to join us, you know." She invested that last sentiment with false snobbery and flicked her upturned nose with an affected forefinger.

"In that case, I would be foolish not to take the opportunity to introduce my daughter to the finest society the region has to offer." He rubbed his fingernails against the lapel of a blazer he wasn't wearing and then inspected them with a pretend satisfied air.

"Indeed." She sniffed, enjoying their silliness.

"I'm assuming then, that my fine daughter will find a place in your esteemed school so she can hone the fine manners expected of a lady of her station."

"Of course." Lydia sobered, hoping she wouldn't regret her decision.

Lydia's neighbor Georgia sat at the cloth-covered kitchen table, where she and Lydia had been chatting as Georgia borrowed a cup of flour. Lydia had hoped her neighbor might have a clue about Lydia's secret admirer, but her speculation had revealed little.

Georgia ran a red fingernail over the image on the ornament sent from Lydia's secret admirer. "So you think Drake sent you this?"

"Who else? After all, it arrived just before he did."

"And it was postmarked Independence."

"Yes. He could have stopped off there to mail it so I wouldn't catch on. Trouble for him is, I did."

"You could ask him, you know."

"I've thought about it, but the time never seems right. And what if I'm wrong? I'd really look like an egotistical idiot."

"You're wise to be cautious. I don't think it's Drake." Georgia set the ornament on the table. "I think he's smarter than that. If it had been Drake, he would have mailed the ornament well before he left town so you wouldn't know it was from him."

"But if it's not from Drake, then who?"

"Ralph."

The high volume of Lydia's laughter surprised even her. "I appreciate the belly laugh, but you've got to be joking. Ralph?"

"Yes, Ralph. I've seen how he flirts with you. If he stayed at everyone's house as long as he does with you, it would take him two days instead of one to finish his route."

Lydia made a tossing motion with her hand. "You've got to be nuts, Georgia. Ralph is just being friendly. I'll bet he tells all the women on his route how pretty they are."

"Pretty? He tells you that?"

Lydia wished she hadn't blurted out the fact. "Yes. But I think nothing of it. He's just passing the time of day."

"That's what you think. He never tells me I'm pretty. Case in point."

A quick glance Georgia's way told the tale. The striking redhead never left her house without appearing immaculate and fashionable. Her willowy yet curvy build always attracted the admiring looks of men and envious glances from women.

"There's too much competition for your attention," Lydia speculated. "He must think he has a better chance with someone plain like me."

"Plain? When was the last time you looked at yourself?"

She felt a blush. "You'll say anything to make me think it's Ralph, won't you?"

"He's secure, stable, and has a reliable job. A girl could do worse."

"Yes, he is all those things, and nice, too. But would you settle for that yourself?" Lydia paused. "No, you wouldn't. And if you had, you'd be married by now."

"This is true."

"Besides, it can't be Ralph. You should have heard him go on and on about how the person violated everything decent in the world by not including a return address." She giggled.

"Ah, then he protested too much?"

Lydia squirmed. "I didn't think of it that way."

Georgia pointed at Lydia. "See there? I told you. It has to be Ralph. He's your secret admirer. Well, not so secret, really."

"We'll see. Maybe my admirer, whoever he is, will send something else that will offer me a better clue."

"You really want it to be Drake, don't you?"

"No!"

"Ah, now who is protesting too much?" Georgia sighed. "If I were you, I'd forget Drake. Maybe he's still handsome and all that, but I remember you weren't so happy with him after what he did. And if not for that, he would never have left town and married someone else."

Georgia spoke in a matter-of-fact way, but her words cut Lydia to the quick. "He says he's changed. He was even wearing a cross."

"Oh, is that so? Well, it's been a long time, but I believe people are born with certain personalities and they may alter their habits, but they will always be who they are no matter what. So I would be careful if I were you. I care about you. That's the only reason I say that."

"I know. I wouldn't take the advice of any other woman so close to heart. I know you want what's best for me."

"I do. So what did you decide about his daughter? Please

tell me you didn't take her in your class."

Lydia clenched her teeth and formed her mouth into a sheepish curve. "Well. . ."

Georgia groaned.

"She really needs me."

"I hope you're not just telling yourself that."

"No. She really does. You should have seen the way she was dressed for the party. And her makeup! Her lipstick was almost black."

"I've seen that look before." Georgia wrinkled her nose. "I don't like it."

"At least she's willing to wear makeup."

"But you know how it is. She will have just as much trouble getting used to not wearing so much makeup as someone who wears none has trouble getting used to seeing color on her face. Do you really think you'll be able to get her to tone it down?"

Lydia knew what Georgia meant. She had taken on a girl with a similar appearance three years before and, in spite of repeated lessons on tasteful and proper cosmetic application, the girl returned to her former look the next day. "All I can do is try. But there's more to this than makeup."

"I'll say."

"Look, I don't care who her father is, this girl needs help. She has no mother, she's not close to her grandmother, and she hasn't made friends here yet. Through Charming Manor, she can make nice friends and get the support she needs to make a better life for herself."

"So you are being charitable. Good for you."

Lydia wouldn't have tolerated such a snide remark from anyone but her best friend. "I am, as a matter of fact. But I have to say, I see something in Kelly that I'm not sure others do. Not that she seems easy to like. At least, she hasn't been so far. But she can change. I just know it."

"All I can say is, I wish you well."

Chapter 4

Lydia slid into the pew beside Drake. Kelly was on his other side. A mishap with her cat Scarlett had delayed Lydia, so she barely had time to greet them before the service began. As she swayed to the music and sang familiar lines, guided by the words on the screens, Lydia forgot about her cares and focused on God. Still, she took comfort in Drake's presence beside her as the minister spoke about references to the harvest season found in scripture, focusing on the apostle Paul's letter to the Romans, in which he wrote of his desire to reach his brothers for Christ, adding to his harvest among the Gentiles.

Lydia wondered who had been responsible for Drake's conversion. Or was Georgia right? Had Drake never really changed? Judging from Kelly's appearance, she didn't look as though she had grown up under strong Christian influence. Or maybe her obvious rebellion was a sure sign that she had indeed.

Lord, give me wisdom.

After the service they walked together to their cars. Lydia couldn't resist noticing the teenager. To her relief, she had forgone the rock star T-shirt and was wearing one depicting an angel instead.

"So you like angels?"

"No, I'm just wearing this because I don't like them."

"Kelly!" Drake's mouth formed itself into such a straight line that it nearly disappeared. His ebony eyes became hidden under narrowed lids.

"Ask a stupid questio—"

"Kelly, we are still on church grounds," Drake reminded her.

Kelly blanched. "Okay, I'm sorry, Miss Lydia. I was just joking."

"I understand." Lydia bit her lower lip to keep from adding a curt remark that sarcasm doesn't become a lady and is rarely funny. She had to remember that if she wanted a relationship with the girl that could change her life for the better, she would have to become more than just her charm school instructor. This meant she couldn't take advantage of every chance to correct Kelly. "I suppose I could have asked a more intelligent question, or simply complimented your shirt. And I *do* like it."

Kelly's sour look faded into a slight grin before she seemed to remember herself and put her hard mask back on.

Drake stopped behind a sensible Ford that Lydia guessed was several years old. "So where is your car?"

Lydia looked over the horizon. "At the far end of the lot. Serves me right for being late." She shrugged. "I guess I'd better be going."

"Got any plans?"

Lydia wasn't sure how to answer. She didn't have anything more pressing to do than read the Sunday newspaper. Yet even though the last few weeks had been pleasant and she hadn't received any more mysterious gifts, she wasn't sure how far she wanted to take a renewed friendship with Drake. A glance at Kelly gave her the answer. "Nothing too special."

"Good. Want to eat dinner with us?"

How could she answer without sounding self-righteous? "I, uh, I usually try not to eat out on Sundays. Or shop or anything like that." She nodded once toward the church. "Pastor Bart suggested we just rest on Sundays, and I've found his advice to be such a blessing."

"Oh, I wasn't inviting you out. Mom has dinner fixed for us at home. So if you're allowed to eat with friends on

Sunday, I know she'd be glad to see you again."

Lydia swallowed. She hadn't seen Mrs. Kingston outside of a crowded public setting since senior year. Since then they had exchanged pleasantries from time to time, but never talked. Not as they once shared their hopes and dreams together. What did Mrs. Kingston think of her? She had liked her, but that was years ago, before the breakup. She wasn't sure she wanted to face her in her own home. "I, uh—"

"Oh, come on. Why, she'd have my head if she thought I'd sat right by you in church and didn't invite you for dinner. And if she found out I invited you and you didn't take me up on it, she'd be liable to come by your house and get you."

Lydia could imagine Mrs. Kingston taking such action. The thought brought on a chuckle. "In that case, it sounds like I'd better go along."

"So how was the sermon?" was the first statement out of Mrs. Kingston's mouth when they arrived at the Kingston home. The house was just as Lydia remembered—cozy and smelling of pine cleaner.

"It was good, Mom."

"That's what I figured. The Bible's only so big. How many sermons can you get from it?" She eyed Lydia. "Oh, I didn't know you brought a guest."

Lydia couldn't tell from the older woman's expression whether she was glad Lydia was present or not. "Nice to see you again, Mrs. Kingston. I appreciate your willingness to include me today."

"Think nothing of it. It's been a long time."

"Yes, ma'am." She wanted to add "too long" but resisted the urge. "Now what might I do to help you?" She realized she should have brought a hostess gift for Mrs. Kingston—perhaps a loaf of homemade bread or cookies—but Drake's off-the-cuff invitation had left her without time to prepare a suitable gift.

"Not a thing. Now you sit right on down. Kelly helped me set the table before she left this morning. She can get the things to the table now for me. Can't you, Kelly?"

Kelly gave a halfhearted nod but acquiesced.

As they feasted on fried chicken, mashed potatoes, sliced tomatoes, fresh green beans, and cherry pie, the conversation was surprisingly easy and friendly. Every now and again she caught Drake looking at her in a wistful way. She wished he wouldn't. She wasn't ready for a trip down memory lane.

Neither was his mother, apparently. Mrs. Kingston's voice didn't hold quite as much warmth and her smile wasn't quite as deep as it had been in years past. She had every right to be wary. Perhaps she didn't want to get her hopes up for Lydia and Drake—again.

A few days later, Ralph knocked on the door. Lydia wanted to duck and pretend she wasn't home but knew she had to answer.

"Hi, Miss Lydia." His smile was broad as usual.

She didn't have the heart to leave him standing in the rain. "Come on in."

"Don't mind if I do."

Now that Georgia had speculated the unthinkable—that Ralph was her secret admirer—she wished he didn't feel so at home. Thankfully, he didn't wait for her to express any assurances.

"I have another package for you. This time it's too big for your box. So I thought you'd like to have it now, inside, especially since it's raining." He peered through her living room window framed by transparent white lace curtains. Lydia remembered that she needed to change her curtains and rugs to reflect the transition from summer to fall. She watched his gaze travel to the rose-patterned rug. "Glad it's not raining heavy yet. I'd hate to track in on all your pretty rugs. You always keep such a spotless house, Miss Lydia. Always as pretty as you are."

"Thank you, Ralph." Her voice sounded less grateful than she meant. Still, she didn't add any remarks, not wanting to encourage him more than she apparently already had.

He handed her a box so large she knew she would have to sit down to open it. Yet its dimensions defied its light weight.

"What could it be?"

"I don't know but again, there's no return address. And you know how I feel about that. It must be from that secret admirer of yours."

Did he know because he was sending the packages himself? Or was he just curious? She studied the address label and contemplated whether to come up with an excuse not to open the box right away.

Ralph eyed the brown wrapping. "It's postmarked Kansas City this time. Seems whoever it is stays on the move."

"Kansas City and Independence are not that far from each other," she pointed out. "You should know that yourself."

"Yep. Haven't been to either place lately, though."

"Oh." She wondered if he was saying that just to give her a false reassurance. Whatever his motives, she could tell he wasn't about to budge until she opened it. Rather than argue, she decided to humor him.

Before long she had opened the box and withdrawn a lovely silk flower arrangement of white poinsettias.

Ralph whistled. "Wow, he didn't spare any expense."

"I didn't think you'd know about such things, Ralph," Lydia noted.

"I hope you aren't calling me a cheapskate, Miss Lydia."

"Not at all. I mean, I didn't think you would know about silk flower arrangements."

"Oh. Well, I took one to a sick friend recently. You know her. Opal Kingston."

"Oh. Why, of course I know Mrs. Kingston."

"I met her playing bingo at the hunt club. She won two hundred dollars that night. She's a right nice woman. She's had hip replacement surgery, you know."

"Yes, I know."

"I was taking her to the doctor before her son and granddaughter got back here to help. They're a little late, though. She's walking just as well as you and I do. I think she likes the company, though. I understand her granddaughter is taking classes with you."

"Yes."

"Well, if anybody can get her straight, you sure can." Ralph eyed the flower arrangement. "This guy has a thing for Christmas, doesn't he?" He looked back out the window. "That sky's looking mighty ominous. I'd better get going."

She set the box aside with one hand and held the arrangement with the other, rising from her seat. "Have a good day, Ralph."

As she watched him depart, she felt more puzzled than ever.

A month later, Lydia looked over the girls who sat around her living room. The class had proven to be one of her favorites. Jennifer no longer appeared snobbish, and Genna had become much more polished. But Kelly still seemed rebellious. She had responded in a lukewarm manner to her makeover lesson, using darker shades with a heavier hand than Lydia recommended. Lydia took a small amount of satisfaction in the fact Kelly had moved to a softer color palette that brought out her gorgeous complexion and shiny dark hair. Her attitude had softened some, but she could still be surly. Lydia knew better than to expect a change overnight, but she couldn't help feeling discouraged at times.

Lydia didn't dare tell Kelly she'd been praying for her.

"Your assignment for this week was to write a bread-and-butter note," she reminded her students. "I am very pleased with what you all wrote." She held up a flower-embossed note. "I have one I'd like to read aloud."

The girls looked at each other, each obviously hoping hers was the chosen note. Lydia read:

Dear Dominick,

Thank you for the wonderful hospitality you presented me with at your house last evening. The escargot, the filet mignon, the chocolate mousse—all were beyond words. I can't believe you flew in a chef all the way from Paris to prepare our meal!

And the gorgeous diamond pendant from Tiffany's? What can I say? I will treasure it always.

Again, thank you for your hospitality. I look forward to jetting off with you to Jamaica next week.

XOXOXO,
Kelly

As she read, groans and giggles filled the living room. But when the others discovered that Kelly had written the letter, some gasped while others nudged her.

"Is that really a bread-and-butter letter?" Jennifer asked. "It sounds more like an engagement letter to me."

Lydia smiled. "Yes, it does sound like this couple is romantic, but as far as thanking him for his hospitality, it meets the requirement. Kelly, I give you an A-plus for creativity."

Kelly beamed for a split second before turning her mouth into an upside-down U. "Yeah, so what? I thought you'd flunk me."

"Flunk you? Of course not. Besides, no one here is a failure," Lydia assured them. "We are all winners."

Kelly sent her stare to the ceiling and crossed her arms.

Lydia suppressed a sigh.

Stick with me, Lord. I need You.

Ralph sauntered up to the door, right on time. "You got another one of those packages, Miss Lydia. Postmarked Independence again. Sure you don't know anybody there?"

"No, I don't."

"Well, somebody there sure seems to like you a lot. Why don't you open it up and see what's inside?"

Lydia arched an eyebrow. "I think you're finding this mystery more tantalizing than I do, Ralph."

"Always thought it might be fun to be an amateur detective. Never had occasion to, though. Not much exciting happens around here."

"I can't say that's a bad thing."

"Nope. I suppose not. So are you gonna open the package?" He tapped his foot.

She opened the brown paper and discovered a box wrapped in silver foil. "It's from the same store as before. The Christmas Store." She set the box on the wrought iron table and lifted its heavy contents. She gasped as she unwrapped red tissue paper and revealed a ceramic Christmas tree decorated with painted ornaments. "Isn't it beautiful!"

"Yep. Whoever it is really likes Christmas."

She couldn't resist. "You like Christmas, don't you, Ralph?"

He shrugged. "It's okay. Mainly more work for me, like I said before. But speaking of Christmas, I was wondering if I could ask you a question."

"Certainly." Her stomach lurched. Was he about to invite her to a Christmas party or dance? Or to his house for dinner? She rehearsed ways to say no before he posed his query.

"Well, it's getting pretty close to the holidays and all, and I was wondering if you might have any suggestions as to what I might get for Mrs. Kingston. I know you know her son."

So the word was out. "Um, yes I do know her son. I didn't know you and Mrs. Kingston were such good friends. I'm glad to hear that."

His face flushed. "Yep, she's a mighty fine woman."

A mighty fine woman. He had said something much like that about her in the past. Could it be that Ralph was interested in Mrs. Kingston romantically? Lydia recalled her mentioning Ralph. The idea of such a romance left Lydia with a warm feeling of relief.

"Yes, she is a fine woman," Lydia agreed. "And I do believe I smelled a whiff of gardenia perfume on her the other day. Maybe she'd like a bottle of that."

"I don't know." He wrinkled his nose. "That doesn't sound too practical to me."

"Well, she did say her toaster's on the fritz, but I wouldn't recommend that as a Christmas gift. At least, not for a lady friend." She winked.

"Maybe not. You always know what to do, Miss Lydia."

Dusting her office, Lydia observed the Christmas-related gifts she had received from her secret admirer. They were all so beautiful and thoughtful. "I wonder who you are, Secret Admirer."

At least he wasn't Ralph. She felt certain of that, after their last conversation where he revealed his interest in Mrs. Kingston. "Maybe it *is* you, Drake."

She wished it were so.

And she wished it weren't so.

She picked up the white silk poinsettia. "It will take more than pretty flowers to convince me you've changed, Drake Kingston."

At that moment, the doorbell rang. Lydia glanced at the

wall clock and saw that the hour was early for the postman to be arriving. "Who could that be?"

She answered the door and saw Drake.

"Good. You're up bright and early," he greeted her.

"So are you."

"I was wondering if you'd let me help you pick out your tree."

"Pick out my tree?"

"Uh, yeah. You know. That tradition where you go out and buy a tree and put these colorful things called ornaments on it."

She chuckled. "I didn't know you were even thinking of such a thing." An image of the little tree from her secret admirer popped into her head.

"Huh?"

With his mouth hanging open as it was, Lydia decided not to confront Drake at the moment. "Never mind. Just thinking out loud."

"Well," he said, "I was planning on picking out mine today. I'd be glad to help with yours, too, if you like."

"Kelly doesn't want to help you?"

"She's baking with Mom. Bonding time, you know. They really need it."

She looked at the truck parked in the driveway. "Well, I was planning on going tomorrow, but I think I'd have lots more fun with you today." She headed toward the closet and retrieved her coat. "Okay. Let's go."

Lydia suddenly felt nervous as they drove toward the Christmas tree farm, when she realized they were alone together for the first time since his arrival. He talked easily about his new job at the construction company, about Kelly's new friends at school, about how much she liked the classes at Charming Manor, even about the weather. A casual observer would have assumed they had been friends forever.

"I think we might stay in Missouri," Drake noted as they turned into the entrance of the Christmas tree farm. "She's making good grades at her new school, and she hasn't complained about you putting her through the paces at Charming Manor."

"Really? You might stay here after all?" Her stomach rolled over with a feeling of nervous excitement. To have Drake stay near her forever! Was it too much to ask? What if it were? What if nothing came of their relationship? Suddenly, she realized she didn't want to consider that possibility. Yet the thought that she had developed feelings anew for Drake scared and elated her at once.

"I'm glad Kelly is doing so well here, but doesn't she miss her friends at all? I mean, you said she was having a hard time without them."

"She was at first, and she still struggles a little. But people have been so welcoming here that she seems to be doing much better. I credit you with a great part of her success."

Drake jumped out of the truck and grabbed a small saw from the back. She felt grateful that the necessary motion kept her from having to respond. She had come to appreciate Kelly over the past months. But would saying so make her seem cloying? Better not to make her feelings known too soon.

She exited the truck. Surrounded by evergreens of all shapes and sizes, she felt eager to find just the right one for her living room. The temperature had dropped but the significance of the cold didn't hit her until they'd been out awhile, walking amid the trees.

"I—I'll take that one." Shivering, she pointed to a balsam that looked to be about nine feet in height.

"Are you sure? Or are you just wanting to get out of the cold?"

"A little of both," she admitted.

"I think this one looks just fine." With several swift strokes, he felled the tree. "I'll take the one beside it. What do you think?"

"It's lovely."

Drake was just as efficient in felling the second tree. Together they dragged their picks to the checkout line.

The farmer scratched his beard. "Two trees? And this

ig? You two must have a mighty big house."

"Oh, we don't—" Drake protested.

"We're not—" Lydia added.

The two stopped in mid sentence and laughed.

The farmer tabulated their bill. "That's a shame. You two ook like you'd make a mighty fine couple."

Lydia was so chilled she was almost grateful to feel heat ise to her face. She noticed Drake didn't seem embarrassed.

"Feel like stopping off for a cup of hot chocolate on the vay back?" he offered.

"Won't you let me make you some at home?" she counered. "It seems like the least I can do after you were so kind o help me with my tree."

"You might not say that when you find out all I can do s help you get yours propped up in the stand before I head out. I still have to get Mom's tree in the house." He pulled he car into the parking lot of the diner. "I definitely want to ake a rain check on your invite for cocoa at your place. But I've been wanting to see if the cocoa at Mildred's Diner is as good as it used to be."

"I think it is, but I'm willing to find out." She glanced at the trees in the back of the truck. "Are you sure your mom won't mind waiting?"

"Nah. She's tied up with all that baking. I doubt she misses me at all."

When they entered the diner moments later, Lydia was almost sorry she took Drake up on his offer. All heads turned when the bell on the door rang to signal their entrance. Most of the other diners turned back to their meals and snacks but others—especially those who had known Drake and her for years—raised their eyebrows.

I guess this is what you call "going public" with a new relationship—or a renewed relationship. I wonder how Drake feels.

He didn't seem to mind, acting as though he were doing nothing more than he did on any other day.

That's just what he thinks. I'm just a friend. This is nothing more than a normal stop at the diner for him.

As they waited for their order to arrive, Lydia chastised herself so much that she could barely register what Drake said. She noticed he flitted from one topic to another without much pause until he tried the cocoa. "Mmmmm. This cocoa is just as good as ever. Even better."

She took a sip of hot liquid, letting the whipped cream topping hit her upper lip. Rich sugary beverage filled her mouth. She swallowed. "You're right."

"How many times did we come here when we were in high school?"

"I can't count them all." She wished her voice hadn't taken on a wistful tone.

"But we can't live in the past. We must live in the present.

That's why it's called the present. It's a gift."

A gift. From my secret admirer?

Yet something stopped her from expressing her thought.

"Yes, life is a gift. And I want to live life to the fullest," he said.

"Really? You seem scared to me."

"No I'm not." She took a sip of her drink to keep from answering further.

"I hope you aren't. Because life is too short not to spend whatever's left of it with the right person." He placed his hand on hers. The sensation would have felt comforting on any winter day, but she knew the sparks she felt were from more than a desire for warmth. A tingling darted through her, but the excitement of his touch mingled with an awareness of security she had never before felt in Drake's presence.

Has he really changed, Lord?

Chapter 5

A few days later, Kelly's voice rang out in the Kingston dining room after she bounded in from school. "Dad! Look!"

Drake knew why she was so excited. Kelly had received a package from New York from a street address he didn't recognize. He had been hesitant to pass it on to her. Kelly's old friends weren't above putting a false return address on a package so they could send her—what? Yet if the package proved to be innocent, he would have regretted withholding it from Kelly.

He had fought the temptation not to pass on the package, but to discard it before any harm could be done. Then he wondered if he should have opened it first, and then passed it on to her. Yet either option, while offering him some solace, would have been deceptive. If he chose to be deceptive, how could he expect Kelly not to follow his example? Still, he didn't trust her. Not yet. And he certainly didn't trust her friends. But he had to take a small step before he could take any big ones. He hoped his trust would not prove to be misplaced.

"It's from New York!" Kelly jumped a little, reminding him of Christmas mornings long ago.

"I know. Who do you think it's from?" He tried to keep his voice devoid of suspicion.

"Selena and Scottie, of course! Didn't you read the return address?"

"Yes." He dared not share his reservations, not when she was willing to open the box right in front of him. That showed she wasn't expecting her friends to pull any stunts. He tried not to let his inward sigh of relief reach too deeply into his chest.

Kelly tore open the package and reached into a cloud of white tissue paper. "It's an angel!" She held the angel in her hands and looked at the simple representation, obviously made by the children themselves, as though it were fashioned from 24-karat gold.

He suppressed a breath of relief. "May I see?"

Kelly nodded and handed him the angel. The little figure was composed of an inverted plastic funnel with pretty material over it to make a gown. Her arms were in a praying position, and she held a book in her hands. At her waist was a gold ribbon. White feathers were glued to her back to give her wings. He tapped on her face and assumed it to be a Styrofoam ball wrapped in light colored material. The children had drawn a face on it with a fine-tip marker. They had spared no ink to depict long lashes. Red lips smiled to create a serene expression. A strawberry red tassel for her hair matched her dress. He had a feeling the choice of color was no coincidence. A halo and collar were made from gold tinsel and what looked like one of his mom's doilies was draped over the skirt.

He ran his hand over the silky, yarn-like hair. "She's beautiful, Kelly."

Kelly nodded. "They know how much I like angels." She took the angel as Drake handed it back. He noticed tears in her eyes.

"What's the matter?"

"No—nothing."

"But you're crying."

"Am not."

"Are, too." He kept his voice gentle.

She sniffled as she stared at the gift from a child. "Someone does care about me, after all."

"Of course someone cares about you. We all care about you, Kelly. Don't you know that?"

She shrugged. "I—I guess." Kelly looked into his eyes. Her soft expression reminded him of the little girl he once knew. "You know what? Hardly anybody has been in touch with me since I left New York."

"Don't be silly. You were on the phone all the time."

She shook her head. "You don't understand."

"But—"

"I was fighting with Darrin, all right? Well, mostly fighting. Other than that, everybody else seems to have forgotten I was ever alive."

"Oh, honey." Drake put his arm around her shoulders. As usual, Kelly remained stiff and didn't return his gesture. Still, he sensed she needed a show of his warmth. "You have lots of new friends here. And we'll be staying here long enough for them to be your friends for a very long time."

"Yeah. I guess." She fingered the angel's skirt. "But I was praying to God that someone back home would still care about me. And they do. Selena and Scottie."

"Of course they do, Kelly."

"So God heard me. I guess that means He does care. He really does."

The end of the first semester had arrived and with it, the

Christmas party. Lydia always held her celebration before school dismissed for the holiday. All of the girls had performed well on the rudimentary aspects of becoming ladies of charm and poise. The following semester would prove a bit more challenging as they learned finer points, including how to cook mouthwatering appetizers and how to host a party. As a preview she had put the girls in charge of some aspects of the Christmas party.

Looking around the house, she noted professionals couldn't have delivered better results. Pine garland framed each interior entrance, filling the house with a fresh scent that mixed well with the enticing aroma of hot spiced apple cider simmering on the stove. Gold tapered candles lent soft light to the generous living room and adjacent dining room. The Christmas tree she and Drake had selected looked perfect in front of the picture window, lit as it was with white lights.

With the room nearly filled with people talking, Lydia could see the party was well on its way to success. Still, she always felt a twinge of nervousness before each class event lest anything went awry. Since she was their teacher, she felt any failure on the part of her students as her own.

Kelly walked into the living room, with Drake close behind her. Lydia swept her gaze to him. His glance caught hers, a shy smile touching his lips. She could see that he was just as nervous for Kelly as she was. Though Kelly had little to fear, judging by her surprisingly stellar performance in class, she could understand a parent's desire to see his daughter succeed. He had dressed the part, wearing a striking combination of color—a dark suit, white shirt, and red tie.

"Kelly, you look absolutely beautiful. I've never seen you look more lovely." It was true. She was wearing a dress in a deep maroon instead of her usual black shirt and jeans. The streak of burgundy in her hair was gone—an irony since the color would have matched the dress to perfection.

In an unusual move for her, Kelly didn't hesitate to greet Lydia right away.

"You seem to be in a good mood," Lydia noted.

"I am. I got an early Christmas gift today. From friends in New York."

"Oh." Lydia suppressed a worried look. Such a good mood could only be attributed to more contact from the boyfriend back in New York; the one Drake thought was a poor influence.

Lord, let me be wrong about this. Don't let Kelly go against her father.

"It's not what you think. I got an angel tree topper from a little girl and boy I used to babysit."

"Oh!" Lydia's hand clutched her chest as though it had a mind of its own before she realized she had shown too much relief.

Kelly giggled. "Had you worried there for a minute, didn't I?"

"I'm afraid so."

"Selena is the one I've been practicing my everyday letters on."

"She's the one who sent you the tree topper." Lydia smiled.

"Yes. Her and her brother Scottie. I knew you'd approve." Kelly's voice held something in it that Lydia hadn't expected—a tone that told her Kelly desired her approval. "Want to see the tree topper?" Kelly didn't wait for an answer, but took the little angel out of its box and showed Lydia.

"She's lovely. Selena must have had some help."

"I think she did. She printed on the card that someone named Noelle showed her how to make it, and Scottie also signed the card. And someone named Todd, too. I guess Todd and Noelle must be friends of the kids' mom." Kelly rolled her glance Lydia's way. "And yes, I will be writing her a thank-you note. Tomorrow."

"Good. Why don't you go her one better? I can give you some of the angel cookies to send to her as a thank-you gift in a pretty Christmas tin. I have some tins left over that I haven't put out and I would be pleased if you took one."

"You do? Are you sure?" She let out a little gasp and widened her dark eyes.

"I'm sure."

At that moment, a couple of the other girls surrounded Kelly, curious and wanting to admire the tree topper. Lydia felt a tug on her arm.

"She sure is excited, isn't she?" Drake asked.

"Yes. She has reason to be. She's received a lovely gift from a friend and she has been a superb student in my classes."

"Believe it or not, her attitude seemed to soften when she got the package."

"I can tell. Her face is glowing." Lydia let out a mock sigh. "And to think I believed the change was due to what she learned at Charming Manor."

Drake lifted his forefinger and pretended to be an old-fashioned etiquette expert. "Poise and charm help one in any endeavor."

Lydia chuckled and watched Kelly talking to the other girls. "Do you know if she hangs out with the same friends at school as she does here?"

"They seem to be calling each other and chatting on the computer a lot."

"Good." Lydia excused herself so she could mingle with the other guests. As much as she wished she could focus her attention solely on Drake all night, she knew she couldn't. Not if she wanted to stay in business.

During the party, she caught Drake studying her on several occasions. Whenever her gaze caught his, he looked away. Could he suddenly be shy after all this time? Or was he sorry he ever took her out to find a tree and then to the diner? She recalled his near confession. Did he still care about her? He seemed as though he did. But she couldn't let him have her heart. Not again.

She noticed Kelly taking a call on her cell phone. Didn't she realize that was a definite violation of manners? Lydia resolved to go over cell phone etiquette again with the girls.

Later, after the party, Lydia summoned Kelly into the kitchen. "Here are the cookies for Selena." She noticed too many were left for her to consume by herself. "Will you allow me to pack you another box for someone else? Darrin, maybe?"

"Darrin," Kelly whispered. To Lydia's shock, tears filled her eyes and trickled onto her cheeks.

Lydia held out a consoling arm. "What's wrong?"

Lydia kept her emotions in check until that moment, when she exploded into sobs. "He—he broke up with me."

"What?"

"He texted me during the party."

"You mean he sent you a text message on your cell phone?" Lydia asked.

Kelly nodded. "How lame is that?"

"Pretty lame. So did he give you a reason?"

"He says he met someone else." Kelly's mouth formed a sneer and her voice betrayed her anger. "He didn't waste any time."

Lydia strode over to her and put a consoling arm around her shoulders. "Oh, honey. I'm so sorry. But you know what?" Lydia stared straight into Kelly's dark eyes. "You've changed so much since you moved here. You've grown into a beautiful young woman that any guy would love to have as a girlfriend. I have to wonder, do you really think you and Darrin still have enough in common to sustain a meaningful relationship?"

"I—I don't know," Kelly admitted.

Lydia had been working with teens long enough to tell what Kelly's tone of voice meant. "Are you really saying that you wish you were the one who broke up with him instead of him breaking up with you?"

"Maybe a little bit." Kelly's chuckle was bittersweet. "But are you really sorry?"

"Sorry you broke up? Probably not. Sorry to see you upset? Yes. Definitely."

"Dad will be jumping for joy."

"He won't be happy to see you hurt, honey."

Kelly shrugged. "He'll never understand."

"Ha!" Lydia blurted. "Of all people, your dad should understand."

"Huh?"

"I've never stopped loving him. And I always will." Lydia gasped. She wished she could take back the words. How did she allow herself to express such buried emotion—emotion she didn't realize she still felt? Ever since Drake had breezed back into town, latent feelings had risen to the forefront of her mind, taking her to another time and place. But to express them to his daughter. . .

What was she thinking?

Kelly's eyes widened. She pointed to Lydia. "So you and Dad—well, I knew something was going on between you."

"No, no. I was talking about an old high school romance."

"This has been going on since high school?"

"Well, not exactly. We dated in high school, but that was years ago. And he did marry your mother, of course." Lydia smiled.

"I hope you don't mind if I don't say I'm sorry."

Lydia felt grateful for the levity that took away from her mortification. "For your sake I can't say I'm sorry, either."

Kelly grinned at the compliment before turning serious. "You know, I've been wanting Dad to find someone for a long time. And now that I've come to know you, I think he could do a lot worse."

"Thanks." Kelly diasappeared.

A faint smell of men's citrus cologne wafted toward Lydia. She turned and saw Drake standing in the doorway.

How much did he overhear? Did he hear me tell Kelly I never stopped loving him?

Her first impulse was to ask Drake but she couldn't. She had to retreat. She was too embarrassed to do anything else. "I—I have to tend to the fire." She headed to the living room and stoked the embers even though the time to let it burn out had passed long ago. She couldn't go back in the kitchen. Not now. She stopped stoking and stared at the dying embers.

What a fool I am. Lord, I pray he didn't hear me. And I pray he won't come out here and ask me about it. Let him be more of a gentleman now than he ever was in high school. Let him walk out now and forever hold his peace.

Drake's shadow filled the doorway, illuminated by the kitchen light.

Let him just tell me good evening. Let him tell me Kelly won't be taking classes next semester. Let him tell me the party was a flop. Anything but that he overheard me!

"Lydia?"

Oh, why can't he leave me alone?

She felt she had no choice but to set her face into an expression of interest and look up at him. "Yes?"

"Come and sit with me, will you?" His voice sounded inviting. He sat on the sofa and patted the empty cushion beside him.

She felt she had no choice but to comply. "Where's Kelly?"

"She's still putting away the food for you."

"She doesn't have to do that."

"Yes she does. Isn't it charming for young ladies to offer to help?"

"Yes, but it's not so charming of me to leave her alone to do all the work." She got up. "If you'll excuse me."

He rose. "No, I won't."

She wanted to argue, but the firm tone of his voice stopped her. He reached for her hand, but she didn't accept the gesture.

"I heard what you said to Kelly."

"Everything?"

"Everything. At least, everything that matters to me. I just wish you had confided in me first."

"It wasn't a confidence. I—I didn't know what I was saying. I was just trying to make her feel better, that's all."

"Feel better?"

Lydia wished she wasn't stuck being the bearer of news so upsetting to Kelly but she was grateful that the focus was off her, if only for a moment. "You didn't know her boyfriend back in New York broke up with her?"

"No." His shoulders dropped an inch. "I can see we still have a long way to go as far as getting our relationship to where it should be. I'm glad she has you to confide in. Mom and she have been getting along better, but Kelly still looks at her as someone too old to understand anything."

"Funny. She probably understands more than all of us put together."

"You have to get beyond your teen years to see that, I think."

Lydia nodded. "I wouldn't put too much stock in Kelly confiding in me. I asked her what was wrong and she told me. Besides, I'm sure she would have told you, too, once she got the chance."

"Is that what you think? Don't you remember how she looked just a few months ago? And you have no idea how morose and secretive she was before she left New York. For her to tell any adult anything like that about her personal life shows a huge change in her. A change I'm glad to see." He patted her hand. "A change I credit you for."

"Don't give me all the credit. She's been going to church and making new friends."

He aimed his forefinger at her. "Because of you. And I know she gives you credit, too. I heard how happy she was when she heard your confession."

"There's a big difference between thinking it would be nice for your father to find someone new and the reality if that were to happen. Besides, maybe she was just being nice."

"Another thing no one would have accused her of before." He placed his hand on her shoulder. She tried not to let his touch affect her. She had to protect herself from the ghosts of the past. "But everyone would accuse you of being more than nice."

His words could have been uttered by a casual acquaintance, yet because they came from him, they sent a shiver of happiness through her. She fought her feelings; trying not to remember the day they selected the Christmas tree. She tried not to recall the old flames of the young love they shared so long ago. She tried not to remember how he had broken her heart once. She couldn't let herself be that vulnerable again.

"Lydia, I think you know how I feel about you. It's like I never left."

"Yes. You're right. It's like you never left."

"I'm so happy to hear you say that." His face was lit with love, an expression she remembered all too well. She had seen shadows of such emotion in recent times, but hadn't seen its full flush in a long time. At that moment, she realized how much she missed his love.

She looked over his shoulder, beyond him into the blackness of her backyard. The darkness reminded her of the cold and sent a shiver through her body. She crossed her arms and rubbed her palms against her forearms.

Obviously mistaking her gesture as a plea for his warmth, Drake took her into his embrace. She froze, but he ignored her stiffened body. "I still love you, Lydia. I didn't realize until I came back here how much."

"No." She pulled away. "No. Don't say that."

"Why not?"

"Don't you see? I let you break my heart once. Not again. I'm smarter than I was when I was a teenager. Way smarter." Then why was she talking like a teenager? She clenched her teeth underneath closed lips to keep herself from saying anything more.

"I'm so sorry."

"That I'm smarter?" she couldn't resist quipping.

"No. That I broke your heart as thoroughly as you broke mine."

"Me? How can you even think such a thing? You're the one who was caught stealing, and you're the one who got sent away to military school. I stayed here, by myself. Wishing things could be different. You're the one who left me, by your actions and their consequences. I'll never forgive you!" The strength of her anger surprised even her.

"What do you mean, you'll never forgive me? I'm the one who should be forgiving you."

"What?" She felt her mouth drop so far open it couldn't have stretched another centimeter.

"I wrote to you after I left. I visited you that Christmas. And what did you do? You acted like you never even knew me."

"I—I didn't. Don't you see? You betrayed me! You proved you weren't the guy I thought you were. You never should have stolen from other people. You were nothing more than a common thief!"

He flinched.

"I remember what you told me," she continued, unable to stop herself. "You said it was fine, that those car dealers were covered by insurance and the big companies would be the ones to pay for the stereos and whatever else you took out of the cars on the dealer's lot. But who do you think pays insurance premiums? Why, you may as well have stolen from your own mother!"

"Do you think you're telling me something I haven't heard?"

She realized how self-righteous she sounded. "I guess not. I'm sorry." Embarrassment over just how much resentment she still harbored filled her. She softened her voice. "If only you had stopped to think about what could happen to

you—to us—if you were caught. But you didn't. And onc
you were, it was too late."

"I know that now. But must you lecture me like I'm
a five-year-old? Don't you think I was punished enough
Being sent away like that was bad enough, but losing yo
was more punishment than I ever thought I could bea
And now to have you be so cold after all this time." H
paused. "Even the car dealer forgave me and agreed not t
press charges, and he's the one I really wronged. You know
his forgiveness is one of the main reasons why I came t
a saving knowledge of Christ. He was a Christian, and h
walked the talk. You open and close your classes with praye
encourage your students to enrich their spiritual lives, g
to church. Is your charm—and your spirituality—nothin
more than an act?"

"An act?" At that moment, she came as close to slap
ping Drake as she ever could have. But she stopped hersel
Striking him, whether or not he deserved it, would accom
plish nothing. Instead she clenched her fists by her side
and tilted her chin at him in a way that would have don
the most snobbish member of the Social Register proud. "I'
have you to know that because I have relied on my faith,
have done perfectly fine all these years. God has sent m
many, many people who care about me. Including Kelly
And their feelings toward me wouldn't be sincere if I wer

putting on an act. People can see through those things, you know. Especially teenagers."

His features flinched in an almost imperceptible flash. Lydia should have been satisfied that she had slapped him verbally in a way the back of her hand never could, but revenge tasted more like bile than sugar.

She must have heard her name, because Kelly chose that instant to appear. "Hey, you guys, what's going on out here?"

"Nothing," they answered in unison.

"That means something." Kelly leaned against the door frame and snapped her white cotton dish towel. An expectant light shone in her dark eyes. "Come on. Tell me."

"We've got to go, Kelly."

"No we don't. I don't have school tomorrow. You guys can talk all you want."

"No," they answered.

Lydia managed to regain composure. She rose from her seat. "Thank you, Kelly, but we're quite through."

"Yes. We are." Drake's voice sounded colder than the lighted icicles hanging from her roof. "Come on, Kelly, let's go."

Kelly obeyed but glanced at Lydia one last time as they left. At that moment, Lydia realized that Kelly couldn't regret the exchange any more than she did.

Chapter 6

Traveling home from Lydia's house, Drake wondered about the roller-coaster evening. First he had been a happy party guest, then overheard Lydia confess to his daughter that she still loved him after all these years. The revelation took his heart skyward. Just as quickly, Lydia's biting words of unforgiveness took him to the pit of despair, a pit where he remained with no sure way to climb out. How could Lydia have been so unforgiving? Hadn't she seen the change in him from all those years ago?

From the passenger seat, Kelly ventured a query. "Dad, what happened tonight?"

"I don't want to talk about it."

"I'm sure you don't, considering Miss Lydia said you weren't always such an angel yourself."

"She told you that?" He set his gaze on the road, unwill-ing even to glimpse at his daughter. How could Lydia have ruined his credibility as a parent? Why did she have to con-tinue to insult him?

"I guess you're not so righteous after all, huh?"

"So you believe her."

From his peripheral vision, he watched Kelly shrug. "I don't have to believe her. I can ask Granny. I have a feeling she'll be honest with me."

"And to think I actually wanted you to have a good rela-tionship with your granny." He let out a small groan.

"So it's true. What did you do that was so bad?"

"Nothing. Nothing really."

"Something bad enough to get you sent to military school. They're threatening Darrin with that, you know," she snapped.

"It would probably do him good."

"Like it did you?"

He swallowed. "If I hadn't been sent away, I would never have met your mother. And I wouldn't have you, the biggest blessing God ever gave me." He pulled the car into the short drive in front of his mother's house.

"But I won't be here forever. In just a few years, I'll be gone."

Drake clenched his teeth under closed lips to keep from

howing his emotion. True, he had Kelly for a few more years, but then she would have to fly out of the nest. He put the gearshift into park and turned off the engine. He took a moment to observe his little girl—now on her way to becoming a young woman—and thanked God that by His grace, she had turned from the wayward path she had begun to take in New York. And whether he wanted to admit it or not, he had to acknowledge Lydia's role in Kelly's turn-around.

He didn't exit the car. "Are you really ready for me to have a new romantic relationship?"

"Yes." She looked at her suede-covered feet. "I think."

"That's a definitive answer. Not."

"I wish I had a mom, but I don't. I hardly remember her." Her confession left a lump in his throat.

"I don't mean any disrespect," she said.

"I know." He rubbed her shoulder even though he knew she couldn't sense his touch through her coat. "How can you love someone you know only through old videotapes and pictures?"

"I do love her, in a way," she promised. "It's just that, I think you need someone. Maybe it's not Miss Lydia, but you two seem to like each other. And if you want to marry her someday, I would understand. I don't want to hold you back."

He placed his hand on her knee. "I appreciate that. It took a lot of courage for you to say that."

"What? Since I'm a little girl?" Her teasing tone was laced with seriousness. "I can cope. I promise." She looked out the window. "I coped with being stuck out here in the country, didn't I?"

"I think you kind of like it."

Kelly studied the trees. "Maybe." She shuddered. "It's getting cold. Let's go in."

On Christmas Eve day, Lydia heard the crunch of gravel surrendering to the pressure of tires on her driveway.

"Must be Ralph." She set down her dish towel and walked to the living room. Mail volume had diminished to almost nothing in the past two weeks now that staffs at catalog companies assumed all Christmas orders had been placed. A few cards trickled in each day. She looked forward to taking a break with a cup of herbal tea and reading the news from far-flung friends and former students.

"Looks like you got another one of those packages." Ralph handed her a small box. "Seems to me this secret admirer thing has gone on long enough. He needs to make himself known, don't cha think?"

"Yes, it would be nice. Speaking of admirers, how are things with you and Mrs. Kingston?"

He blushed, and not from the cold air she was sure. "Just dandy. I took your advice and got her some flowerdy perfume the clerk at the store said was popular now. I hope she likes it."

"I'm sure she will." Lydia smiled. And to think she had once considered Ralph might be her admirer. Praise the Lord that Ralph couldn't hear her thoughts. She'd be too embarrassed for words. She fingered the package. "This one doesn't weigh much."

"Maybe your secret admirer is going broke."

"Maybe. I hope not." She opened the outer box and found inside another fashioned of gold cardboard foil, a trademark of her favorite chocolatier. She didn't suppress a triumphant smile. Her secret admirer had to be Drake! The package contained four pieces of exquisite chocolate truffles in a gold box. "Come and meet your secret admirer at 122 England Street at seven tonight."

Ralph let out a low whistle. "Sounds like this is getting serious."

Lydia nodded.

"So you know who it is?"

"I have an idea. But I don't want to say just yet." She bid Ralph farewell as politely but as quickly as she could.

Emotions roiled within her. She was to meet her secret admirer at the Kingston address!

So Drake wasn't mad at her anymore. If he was, he wouldn't keep up this secret admirer subterfuge. Her deceitful heart beat with wild happiness. She didn't want to forgive him, but she knew she had to. The time to forget the past had come and gone. And if she let it slip away, he would be gone forever. She had to keep the date.

Hearing a car pull up in the drive, Drake peered out the window. He watched as Lydia got out. She was so beautiful, as always. Even covered by a full-length black coat with her honey blond hair obstructed by a black hood, he could see her bright face wearing a pleased expression. He felt his heart leap happily into his throat. What was she doing here?

The first thing she did was to offer him a chocolate from a box of four pieces of candy. He accepted a bonbon and let the sweet, creamy, dark goo melt in his mouth. She watched him with the intensity of a person watching the climax of a mystery program. He sensed that she waited for him to say something. What?

"If this is your idea of a peace offering, I'm all for it."

"My idea? I thought it was your idea."

"I don't understand."

"So you mean, you—you aren't the one who sent this candy?"

"No."

"Then you're not my secret admirer?"

"Secret admirer? What are you talking about?"

"The gifts. You didn't send them?"

"What gifts?"

"Well, a little bit before you came back home, I started getting gifts. An ornament, a flower arrangement, candy—all from a secret admirer. They were all Christmas-related. I—I was thinking it might be you."

"Me?"

She looked at the candy she still held. "I remember that you were sent away at Christmas last time. I thought maybe this was your way of saying you were coming home at Christmas. Forever."

"No. You don't mean it. You don't mean you were hoping it was me?"

Her failure to answer emboldened him.

"All right then. It was me."

"Drake. . ." Her tone bespoke an exaggerated warning.

"Oh, all right. It wasn't me. But I wish it was."

"Even after I wasn't very nice to you the other night?"

"I've thought about it. The wounds we suffer with our

first loves cut deeper than anything else we bear, I've come to realize."

"First love." She looked at her toes. "You were mine."

"And you know you were mine." He took her hands in his. "And you still are."

She flinched and pulled her hand away. "I—I want you to know I forgive you. I'm ashamed I have to say such a thing after all these years. If I had harbored a more flexible spirit all along, I would have given myself the gift of peace."

"And marriage?" His voice caught in his throat. Even though he had gone on with his own life, the thought of her with someone else was too much to bear.

She looked him in the eye. "No. I had other chances, but no one else felt so right. I chose to remain single all these years, and I don't regret it. If things had been different, I wouldn't be the person I am today."

"And a wonderful person you are, Lydia Winters. More wonderful and beautiful than I deserve. I'll bet your secret admirer is a better man than I am—and the one you really deserve."

A familiar female voice interrupted. "Is that what you think?"

"Mom!" Drake cried. "How long have you been standing there?"

"Not too long, but long enough." She crossed her arms.

"Drake Kingston, I'm ashamed of you."

"What?"

"To give up this fine woman that easily."

"What do you want me to do, Mom? Figure out who the secret admirer is and beat him up? That would have been the old Drake. He's dead and gone."

"Who says the secret admirer is a man?"

"What!" Lydia and Drake expressed their simultaneous surprise.

"I mean, what if it's someone who admires Lydia in a different way—a former student, or a well-wisher?"

"Oh." Lydia agreed.

Drake thought for a moment and snapped his fingers when an idea entered his mind. "Kelly! It has to be Kelly!"

"Why do you think it's Kelly?" Lydia asked.

"Because she told me she'd like to see us get married someday."

"Married?" Though Lydia seemed surprised, a little smile of pleasure crossed her lips before she set her mouth back in line.

Drake gave himself a mental kick for mentioning the "M" word in such a cavalier manner. He meant to say something to her when the time was right. Then again, the little smile gave him confidence he'd not had previously.

"Hmm. Someday is probably years down the road in her mind."

Leave it to Lydia to be practical. "Maybe," he conceded. "But I have a feeling she wouldn't mind if it were sooner."

"Kelly!" he called toward her bedroom.

"She's not here," Mom said. "She went to the mall with Jennifer and Genna."

"As happy as I am to learn about her feelings, it doesn't matter in the context of the secret admirer. The gifts started arriving this past summer, before we met."

"So then, who?" Drake's eyes narrowed. "I'll bet it's Genna's father. He can't take his eyes off you whenever you're in the same room together."

"No, it isn't him." Mom seemed certain.

"Then who is it?" Drake challenged her.

"It's me."

"What?"

She nodded. "As soon as I learned you were coming back home to take care of me—ostensibly—I knew I had to do something to get you and Lydia back together. Since the first package arrived at her house just before you did, I thought surely she would put two and two together and figure out it was you. That's what I mean. I wanted her to think it was you."

"Mom!"

"I would have never guessed," Lydia added. "When I came to dinner that first Sunday, I wasn't even sure you wanted me to be there."

"I have to admit, I had a hard time playing it cool."

"You're quite an actress," Drake said.

"Maybe I missed my calling." She winked.

Drake shook his head and smiled. "You know, Mom, you didn't need to do something so silly. But I love you for it."

"I know. I had no idea you'd end up sending Kelly to Lydia's charm school and take things from there. I might have known you'd have the smarts to figure out a way to get her back on your own."

"But, Mom, I really did want Kelly to go to Charming Manor. And she's all the better for it."

"You're right on all counts. But I know you still love Lydia. Mind you, I thought the world and all of Mandy, and I wouldn't take all the money in the world for Kelly. But if things had been different back when you two were in school, you would have been married all along. Life is short, Son. I know that since your father died on me way before I was ready. Now you two take this second chance. They don't come around too often." Mist formed in her eyes. A proud woman, she turned her face away and made a quick exit into the kitchen.

"She's right, you know," Lydia said. "Second chances don't come around too often."

"Are you saying you want another chance with me? I can't promise you the perfect relationship. I can promise you

I'll still make mistakes, but hopefully not as bad as the ones I made back in high school."

A wan smile curved her lips. "I can promise you I'll make mistakes, too. I think I've already proven that. All I can do is to say I've learned my lesson. I promise to try not to be so rigid and unforgiving in the future."

"I have a feeling since Kelly is already a teenager, we'll both need to exercise our full capacity for love and forgiveness."

"I want to, Drake." She squeezed his hand in hers. "I really, really want that for us."

"For the three of us."

"For the two of us, first."

"Yes. That is the way it should be." Drake squeezed her hand. "I really do love you, Lydia."

"And I love you, too. I don't think I ever stopped. Not even during those dark days so long ago when you had to leave me."

"I'll never leave you again, I promise. Unless you want me to."

"No, I don't. I know that now."

Drake took her in his arms and kissed her. The touch of her lips proved sweet beyond his wildest imaginings. As he held her, he noticed that Lydia's body was not that of a teenager, but a woman. A woman who loved him. And who always would.

A low whistle interrupted. Drake looked up. "Kelly!"

"It's about time, you guys."

Mom looked in. "I heard a whistle. Does that mean what think it does?"

"Sure does."

Kelly jumped up and down and ran over to them, a surprisingly childish motion for a teenager who wanted to look ophisticated at all times. She hugged them both. "This will e perfect. Almost like the Brady Bunch."

Lydia's laughter tinkled throughout the room. "I'm not so ure we can be called a bunch."

"Okay," Kelly conceded. "So we don't have six kids."

"At least not yet." Drake smiled.

Lydia's blush told him that their minds—and hearts—ad finally become one.

ANGEL SUGAR COOKIES

Be sure to have available cookie cutters in angel shapes or the shape(s) of your choice before beginning.

  1½ cups sugar
  ⅔ cup butter
  2 eggs
  2 tablespoons milk
  2 teaspoons vanilla extract
  3¼ cups flour
  2½ teaspoons baking powder
  ½ teaspoon salt

Cream the butter and sugar together in a large bowl.
Add milk, vanilla extract, and eggs to the bowl.
In a separate bowl, mix the dry ingredients together.
Add the dry ingredients to the bowl of wet ingredients.
Mix on medium speed for about two minutes, or until
    ingredients are combined.
Shape the finished dough into a ball and wrap it in plas-
    tic wrap.
Refrigerate overnight.

Ready to Bake:

Preheat oven to 400 degrees F.

Lightly grease the cookie sheets if they are not nonstick.

Roll out the dough, (half at a time) until the dough is ¼ inch thick.

Shape with cookie cutters.

Bake for 9–11 minutes or until the edges turn golden.

ICING:

1 cup confectioners sugar

2 teaspoons milk

2 teaspoons light corn syrup

¼ teaspoon almond extract

3–4 drops food coloring as appropriate to the shape of your cookies

Mix the confectioners sugar and the milk together in a small bowl until smooth.

Add the almond extract and the corn syrup.

Mix well.

Dip cookies or paint them with icing.

TAMELA HANCOCK MURRAY

Tamela Hancock Murray is an award-winning, best-selling author of twenty Christian romance novels and novellas and seven Bible trivia books. She lives in Northern Virginia with her godly husband and beautiful daughters who keep her busy with church and school activities. When she and her husband married over twenty years ago, the bottom layer of their wedding cake was baked into the shape of a three-leaf clover.

Tamela loves to hear from her readers! Send e-mail to Tamela@TamelaHancockMurray.com.

A Letter to Our Readers

Dear Readers:

In order that we might better contribute to your reading enjoyment, we would appreciate your taking a few minutes to respond to the following questions. When completed, please return to the following: Fiction Editor, Barbour Publishing, Inc., P.O. Box 719, Uhrichsville, OH 44683.

1. Did you enjoy reading *One Christmas Angel*?
   ❑ Very much—I would like to see more books like this.
   ❑ Moderately—I would have enjoyed it more if _____
   _____
   _____

2. What influenced your decision to purchase this book?
   (Check those that apply.)
   ❑ Cover   ❑ Back cover copy   ❑ Title   ❑ Price
   ❑ Friends   ❑ Publicity   ❑ Other

3. Which story was your favorite?
   ❑ *Strawberry Angel*   ❑ *Angel Charm*

4. Please check your age range:
   ❑ Under 18   ❑ 18–24   ❑ 25–34
   ❑ 35–45   ❑ 46–55   ❑ Over 55

5. How many hours per week do you read? _____

Name _____

Occupation _____

Address _____

City_____ State _____ Zip_____

E-mail_____

If you enjoyed

ONE CHRISTMAS ANGEL

then read:

A Time for Angels

Making and Giving Away Angels
at Christmastime Sets Love in Motion
for Two Couples

Angel on the Doorstep by Sandra Petit
An Angel for Everyone by Gail Sattler

If you enjoyed
ONE CHRISTMAS ANGEL
then read:

patchwork CHRISTMAS

one woman's Legacy of hope
is bestowed upon two
struggling couples

Remnants of Faith by Renee DeMarco
Silver Lining by Colleen L. Reece
